"Is Ellis your latest lover?"

Blase's question made Merrin feel like slapping his insolent face, but prudence dictated a wiser course.

"That's no business of yours," she said distantly, setting off past him toward the house.

Blase's hand on her arm was brutal. "Tell me, damn you!"

"Why don't you watch and see?" she taunted. "And let me go! I hate your touch!"

Blase smiled, his sensuous fingers clasping her even tighter. "Why did you come back, Merrin?" he asked, his glance cold and hard.

"Ellis needed me." She was mesmerized by his eyes, unable to look away, unable to lie.

His fingers increased their insistent pressure.

"And do you give Ellis *everything* he needs, my wanton?" he hissed.

Books by Robyn Donald

HARLEQUIN PRESENTS

HARLEQUIN ROMANCES

These books may be available at your local bookseller.

For a free catalog listing all titles currently available,
send your name and address to:

Harlequin Reader Service
2504 West Southern Avenue, Tempe, AZ 85282
Canadian address: Stratford, Ontario N5A 6W2

ROBYN DONALD

an old passion

Harlequin Books

TORONTO • NEW YORK • LONDON
AMSTERDAM • PARIS • SYDNEY • HAMBURG
STOCKHOLM • ATHENS • TOKYO • MILAN

Harlequin Presents first edition December 1983
ISBN 0-373-10649-1

Original hardcover edition published in 1982
by Mills & Boon Limited

Printed in U.S.A.

CHAPTER ONE

IT was, Merrin Sinclair decided, a very pleasant day, the first of autumn, crisp, clear and still beautifully warm. Summer's heat and humidity had gone and winter's fogs and chills were far enough in the future to be disregarded. And although it was her first day back at work after a very pleasant holiday spent lazing on the beach at Whitianga there was no cause for complaint in that. As secretary and right-hand woman to an author she enjoyed her work immensely. Not to put too fine a point on it, Ellis Kimber was a darling, and his thrillers entertaining and well written.

Merrin smiled a greeting at an elderly woman over a border of superb dahlias, breathing deeply of the warm air as she turned off the footpath into a driveway. Why Ellis chose to live in this small Waikato town no one knew, unless it was because of its peace and beauty.

Certainly that was why Merrin liked it; in the five years she had lived here she had become a part of the community, accepted, thoroughly at ease. At first a sanctuary, she now considered it her home and knew that she would be content to live the rest of her life there.

'My dear, you look entrancing!' Ellis greeted her with his usual enthusiasm. 'What a superb suntan! How was Whitianga?'

'Blissful.'

He laughed, pushing back the lock of dark hair which flopped on to his forehead. 'Good. So you're ready for another year's hard graft. Merrin, I have the most exciting news for you! You know I've set this next book on a sheep station in Northland? Well, I decided that it would be the ideal time to take up a long-standing invitation, so pack your bags, my dear! We're going to spend the next few weeks in one of the most beautiful spots in New Zealand with an old friend of mine, a chap I went to school with.'

While talking he had led her into the study, gesticulating widely as she put her handbag down and turned to look at him.

'Sounds fun,' she said lightly, ignoring a faint clutch of fear in her stomach. 'Who is this old school friend?'

'Oh, a magnificent creature, believe you me. You'll probably fall just the tiniest bit in love with him; most women seem to find him irresistible, but I know you, with your impregnable armour.'

Merrin's lips twitched. Ellis found her somewhat of an enigma and never lost a chance to tell her so. 'He sounds insufferably conceited,' she commented.

'No, no, you couldn't call him conceited. Very assured, very sophisticated, with the kind of steely strength which makes him the natural focus for everyone in the vicinity. The sort of person that people instinctively turn to for help, that's Blase.'

'*Blase?*' For a moment the room whirled hideously about Merrin's head. She heard Ellis's startled exclamation as he helped her to a chair, dropping her into it with a jolt which probably did more to bring her back to herself than the brandy he insisted she drink or the wet cloth he spread over her wide forehead.

'I'm all right,' she muttered, putting the barely tasted alcohol on to the desk. 'Did you say Blase? Not by any chance Blase Stanhope? At Blackrocks station?'

'That's him.' Ellis was deprecating and cautious 'Obviously you know him.'

'Yes.' Picking up her bag, Merrin took a handkerchief from it and touched it to her lips. 'Here,' she said after a moment, taking the cloth from her forehead, 'I shan't faint, I promise you. But I can't—I can't go with you to Blackrocks.'

Followed a short silence. Ellis juggled the cloth from one hand to the other as if it burnt his fingers before asking, 'Am I to be given some reason, Merrin?'

'Yes, I owe you that.' She sighed, biting her lip as the memories came flooding back. 'My father was head shepherd at Blackrocks until he—died. After my—after my parents' death the Stanhopes gave me a home. I was sixteen then. When I left school I stayed on as a sort of secretary-cum-housemaid. Mrs Grier—Blase's aunt—was especially kind to me.' A bitter smile twisted her lips. 'They all were.'

'Did you not want to work for them?'

She lifted blind eyes, staring through him. 'Oh, I was happy, idyllically, idiotically happy. But I left just after my eighteenth birthday—under a cloud. Blase thought I'd given the key to the safe to—to someone who'd stolen the wages from it. I couldn't convince him otherwise, and all of the evidence pointed to me. The—other person disliked me for—well, there's no need to go into that now.'

Ellis said firmly, 'Drink up the rest of that brandy. No, I insist. You've had a nasty shock and you need something to bring colour back to your face.'

When he wanted to be he was very firm. And he was right, Merrin had had a shock. As she drank the brandy some sort of composure came back to her. She began to regret having told Ellis even the small amount she had.

'Feeling better now?'

Nodding, she put the empty glass down. 'I'm sorry I was so silly. It's just that—well, I don't want to go back there. I was deeply hurt by Blase's reactions.'

'You were in love with him.'

She smiled with cynical composure. 'Of course. As you said, he's a magnificent creature. Six years ago he was twenty-four and I'd been in love with him for at least six years. People do fall in love before they're physically adult. I loved him when I was twelve and I've never . . .' She stopped, appalled at how she had given herself away.

'And you've never got over it,' Ellis finished softly. 'What about that wedding ring you wear, Merrin?'

Tears filled the deep green depths of her eyes. 'Oh—
God!' The words were wrenched from her in an anguish of spirit she had not suffered for a long time
now.

'You married someone else—presumably a Mr
Sinclair—to try and forget Blase. But it didn't work.'

'No, I cheated poor Paul. He's dead now, and if it
hadn't been for me he would still be alive.' She sprang
to her feet, a wildness driving her towards the wide
glass doors overlooking the green depths of the garden.
'Ellis, I can't go with you, I'm sorry. Too much has
happened—too much bitterness, too much anger and
hate. I've only just acquired some peace. If I go back
there it will be like walking into a furnace. I'll be
stripped of everything, my pride, my peace of mind. I
can't go, please believe me.'

There was a long silence as she rested her forehead
against the cool glass, one hand clenching the curtain.

At last he said slowly, 'There's obviously a lot you
haven't told me. Have you ever told anyone, Merrin?'

'No.'

'Not even your husband?'

'No.' She cleared her throat. 'I—I told him a little. I
didn't lie to him. That was why everything went
wrong—Paul couldn't take it. I should never have
married him.'

'Why did you marry him, Merrin?'

Perhaps it was the brandy, perhaps the relief of at
last unburdening herself to someone who had no personal interest, but she told him. 'Because I was carrying Blase's child and I was desperate.'

She swivelled, head held high, searching the thin,
shrewd face for any sign of contempt.

But Ellis said, compassionately, 'My poor child,
what an incredible mix-up! No wonder you don't want
to go back! I'm sorry I pried.'

'No,' she said, exhausted but still proud. 'In a way
it's a relief. The whole thing was a nightmare and for
years I've thrust it into the dark corners of my mind,

forbidding myself to recall any part of it because it was too painful. Perhaps I should have rung Lifeline or contacted the Samaritans or something, but I couldn't bear to—to remember.'

'And so you have shut yourself away behind barriers, refusing to allow anyone to get close to you.' He smiled rather ironically at her startled expression. 'You've always interested me, Merrin—psychologically, I mean. At first I thought that you would find some young man around here and remarry. You're extremely attractive and you have a charm which is hard to define but very potent. It didn't seem possible that you should prefer to remain single. But you've been here five years now, long enough to get over the death of your husband, and yet there are no signs that you want anything more than the most lukewarm of relationships.' He paused, pushing his hand through the lank lock of hair over his brow. 'You know, it might be a good thing for you to go back, exorcise the ghosts. You could well find that that great love you've nurtured all these years has collapsed into a heap of ashes, leaving you free to begin again.'

'*No!*' She sat down, limp with terror. 'Don't use any of your parlour psychology on me, Ellis. I'm no longer in love with Blase, but I don't want to have anything more to do with the Stanhopes. They poison everything they touch and so do I. Believe me, nothing would give Blase more pleasure than to flay me alive. If you were at school with him you must know that he doesn't forgive or forget easily, and he has a tongue like a whip.' She looked up, pleading for understanding. 'Mrs Grier certainly won't want me there either.'

'You're afraid of them!'

'Too damned right I'm afraid of them.' She laughed with harsh distinctness. 'After what they did—it was Terry Grier who stole the wages money. He waited until I was watching television with his mother before he went to my bedroom and took the key to the safe. I'd been to the bank that afternoon to get the money and locked it away, but Blase was away for the day, so I slipped the key into my drawer until he came home. I left Hope Grier watching television and went to my room. Terry was there, putting the key back.' She took a deep, gasping breath, the colour in her skin fading to a uniform pallor which revealed the clear-cut symmetry of her features.

'And what happened then?'

'He—he kissed me.' Her expression revealed her disgust. 'I hated it—he'd tried before, but I'd always managed to avoid him. This time he succeeded, I was so surprised to see him in my room I didn't resist. He must have seen Blase follow me and stop in the doorway, because he said, "Thanks for getting me the money, sweet." He kissed me again.' She looked down at her hands as they twisted together, the slender strong fingers white at the knuckles. 'Then he said—something—which made it seem that he and I had been lovers as well as . . . as . . .'

'You'd better sit down.' Picking up the brandy bottle, Ellis eyed it with suspicion then said as he waved it at her, 'Here, have some more.'

'I must be drunk already,' Merrin retorted with bitter humour, 'because I'm damned if I know why I'm telling you all this.'

'Knocked off balance. Look, don't go on, if you don't want to.'

'You might as well hear the rest, there's not much. I thought Blase was going to kill us both.' She shivered, remembering. 'He—he stood like—he didn't move, just stood there, clenching and unclenching one fist. I've never been so afraid in all my life. He had such terrific self-control—I'd wondered what he'd be like if he ever lost it—believe me, I'm glad I never saw it! I tried to tell him what had happened, but when he asked Hope Grier she said I'd not been near her all night. So that was that. He believed her, of course, and Terry; after all, they were Stanhopes!' The bitterness she still felt clogged her throat. Lifting her head proudly, she finished in a swift monotone, 'So that was that. Terry left Blackrocks in one hell of a hurry, lit out for parts unknown before Blase changed his mind about killing him. It was a week before I was able to get away. Blase devised some interestingly sadistic ways to pass the time in that week. Anyway, I made it. I took a bus to Tokoroa—that was as far as my money would get me—and found a job as a waitress.'

'Was that where you met your husband?'

She nodded, exhausted by the pain which her memories still had. 'Yes. He was kind, in a brash way. One day he found me crying; I'd just heard that I was pregnant. He said he'd take care of me.' Drawing a deep breath, she said drearily, 'I must have been mad.'

'It didn't work out, of course.'

'No. Oh, he tried, and God knows I tried, but he found the reality too much. He began to drink. I—I lost the baby and he drove the car into the river. It was shortly after that that I saw your advertisement. So—here I am! And that's the story of my life. Short, sordid and besprinkled with deaths.'

'The stuff of all the best tragedies,' Ellis told her absently, adding, 'Did Blase know that you were pregnant?'

'Dear heavens, no!' She smiled with cold sarcasm. 'He'd have thought it was Terry's.'

'Hardly,' Ellis pointed out, frowning. 'Even if he believed Grier's lies he would have realised that there was a possibility that the baby was his. Blase's, I mean.'

'I didn't even realise that I was pregnant until I'd been in Tokoroa some weeks.' A shudder made her hug her arms across her chest as if she was suddenly cold. 'When his pride is hurt your old school friend forgets about being a gentleman. He put me through his version of hell the last week he wanted to break me, you see, but I got away before he did.' The tears gathered; with a harsh sob she collapsed into the chair, put her head in her hands and wept as she had not wept for years, painful rigors tearing at her slender body.

When she had calmed down enough to realise that she was alone in the study she felt as though she had been through some kind of emotional wringer. She was limp, drained of all feelings, and could feel an incipient headache at her temples. Hastily she made her way to the bathroom, washed her face and re-applied make-up, working quickly so that by the time Ellis re-appeared she looked something like her normal self.

He arrived wheeling the tea trolley. 'I made coffee and some sandwiches, to mop up the brandy. And I've been thinking. Would you say you have more self-confidence now than when you left Blackrocks, five years ago, wasn't it?'

'Six. Yes, of course, I've gained in self-confidence.' Merrin looked at him warily.

'Well then, why are you so frightened of them? I've seen you deal more than competently with obnoxious reporters and super-confident young men who try to get you into bed. You've come with me to parties and lunches and lectures and I've never yet noticed you put a foot wrong. Why not go back and show them how wrong they were? You'll have me with you.'

In the end, after two days of almost constant pressure, of the nicest possible kind, she gave in, and then only because she felt guilty about leaving him in the lurch. She owed Ellis such a lot. When she had answered his advertisement she had been in a state of shock, so apathetic that she no longer cared what happened to her. Life, ably helped by her own immaturity and stupidity, had dealt her too many blows. She no longer had the capacity to deal with them.

All of this Ellis had seen. Even then she knew that it was that compassionate, caring heart of his which had seen to it that she got the job above other applicants far better qualified than she. Ever kind, drily amusing, gently reassuring, he had guided her through the first months when she had made mistakes and been so

slow that often he must have wondered just where his
gesture had led him.

It was because she was grateful that she had forced
herself to rise above the hell of pain and disillusion she
was mired in and give of her best; she had gained so
much from him that now, when he needed her, she
could not refuse to go with him to Blackrocks.

They spent a day in Auckland on the way. Merrin
withdrew a large amount of money from her account
and shopped, buying herself the kind of clothes she
had never before dared consider. As she was to return
to Blackrocks it was going to be on something like
equal terms with its owners, and she needed armour.
Their life style was totally removed from hers, and
from most New Zealanders', but she had no qualms
about her ability to cope with it.

It was the thought of Blase that robbed her face of
colour, Blase as she remembered him most vividly. Not
the lover who had shown her that physical love could
give rise to a rapture of the senses almost explosive in
its intensity, but Blase as he had been when he watched
Terry release her from that hateful kiss. For a moment
she had thought he would kill her, but the red glow in
his eyes had faded as his cousin spoke, leaving the hazel
depths icily, implacably contemptuous.

'You little slut!' he had said between his teeth, and
that had been all, but even now she shivered when she
thought of it.

'Cold?' The saleswoman looked vaguely affronted,
but went on, 'You from Australia, dear? Queensland
way, perhaps? That's a lovely tan you've got and that
dress shows it off a treat.'

It did indeed, being white and sophisticated, held
up by two thin straps over her shoulder, the clinging
pleated georgette moulding the slender lines of her
body exactly.

'I'll take it,' said Merrin, before her natural caution
reasserted itself. Well, why not? The whole idea was to
show them all that the girl they had each, in their vari-

ous ways exploited, had come about and made something of herself.

And there was always Ellis, who had promised to defend her. Not that he was any match for Blase who was implacable and ruthlessly clever, but at least his presence would prevent their host from openly showing his hatred. She hoped.

For the rest she chose underwear, expensive and beautiful, suitable for a trousseau, and bought herself a bottle of Opium perfume. As if a perfume, however mysteriously enticing, could be any defence against the Stanhopes! Still, it was something she had been promising herself for a while and she needed all the confidence she could get.

For now as they drove closer and closer to Blackrocks she felt her self-assurance oozing through her fingertips. Indeed, if she hadn't had to concentrate on her driving she would have been shaking with foreboding. Ever since Auckland she had cursed herself for being so stupid as to allow Ellis to sweet-talk her into coming back, putting herself into danger again.

'Do they know I'm coming?' she asked abruptly.

'Well, yes, I imagine they do. They know my secretary is coming and I did mention your Christian name. The Sinclair part could be anyone, but I don't imagine there are many Merrins around.'

She smiled, easing out to pass an immense milk tanker. 'No. So they'll have their stilettos finely honed.'

'Forgive me, but don't you think you may be over-dramatising? The Blase Stanhope I know is an arrogant devil, but wordly, more given to playing sophisticated games with equally wordly women than to stabbing people!' Ellis moved uncertainly, restrained by the safety belt from his usual widely-flung gestures. 'Obviously he behaved badly to you, but I imagine that time has mellowed his attitude. By and large, people don't go around seeking vengeance for supposed wrongs, you know.'

'Of course.' She began to see that any harping on things dead and gone could put Ellis in an extremely awkward position. After all, he was Blase's friend; it would be unforgivable for her to drive a wedge between them. She had no right to expect Ellis to act as a buffer.

'As you say, six years is a long time.' She smiled at him. 'You may be right, this visit could well be a liberating event in my life.'

He was too shrewd to be convinced by her capitulation, but he relaxed. Merrin made a mental vow not to embroil him any further. An intensely private person, she found the recollection of her unburdenings extremely distasteful and could only blame her unusual frankness on the combination of shock and brandy. It wouldn't happen again, she thought, remembering just how much she hadn't revealed.

Beyond Whangarei the main road ran north. After being held up for some miles behind a cattle truck Merrin flicked the indicator, turning right down a road which ducked and dived between hills and small valleys, past farms where stands of puriri and totara trees signified the fertility of the soil. After some miles they began to climb slowly at first and then more swiftly, crossing the range of hills which separated the interior from the coast. The last few miles to the summit were pleasant in the shade of heavy bush where cicadas shrilled their tiny zithers, the noise penetrating to the interior of the car through Merrin's window. The air was sweet and warm; in the north it was still summer.

'Noisy, aren't they?'

Merrin nodded, concentrating. Infinitely better than it used to be, the road still had more than its fair share of hairpin bends and driving on thick gravel and slippery clay made things interesting.

'Blackrocks begins here,' she said after they had reached the summit. 'I'll stop half way down where there's a look-out.'

Ellis was not a good traveller, so he welcomed the

respite, unfolding his length from the car with a sigh of gratitude and pleasure. 'It's beautiful,' he observed moving across the loose gravel to stand looking out across the station. It had rained and the atmosphere was moist and scented against the skin. Merrin took a deep breath and went to stand by him, staring down into the panorama beneath.

'This is all Blackrocks,' she told him quietly. 'There are the rocks themselves, the great cliff of old volcanic stone with the waterfall hurtling over it. The station actually goes over the hills and takes in a valley very like the one we've come through. Blase's father bought that; Blackrocks itself dries out badly in summer, but the Waiora block doesn't so the two work in well together.'

Ellis stood silently, his glance sweeping across the valley from the cliff, stark yet softened by its veil of water and the trees which grew in the crevices in the rocks, down to the sea, and all the green and pleasant land which lay between them. It was very quiet, so quiet that the deep barking of a huntaway could be heard as he worked sheep on a hillside right across the valley. The waterfall became a stream, winding between wooded banks through lush river flats to go out of sight around the base of the range. It meandered over the wide wedge of the valley ending at the coast in a wilderness of swamp and lagoon where ducks and heron made their home. Once someone had advised Blase to drain that area, but he had refused, saying curtly that wetlands were a valuable and rapidly diminishing asset, so the little river made its ancient way to the sea undisturbed.

In summer the lagoon was like a warm bath, protected by a sandspit from the ocean beach where the waves made swimming tougher and more invigorating and incidentally more dangerous. On the spit too, the original cover had been left, tea-tree with its aromatic scent, great flax bushes thrusting their sword-like leaves towards the sky and low shrubby twiners and climbers. To the north was a headland of the same volcanic stone as the Blackrocks, hidden by gnarled old pohutukawa trees. And between the hills and the sea lay the station, remarkably green and lush after the heat and drought of summer, dreaming beneath the sun's kiss, clumps of trees and woodlots giving interest and shelter to the landscape, wire fences as straight and true as Roman roads arrowing across the hills.

'Beautiful,' Ellis said again.

Merrin nodded. She could not trust herself to speak. For years she had dreamed of this view, longed for it with a desire which came close to a sickness. And now here she was, and she could not feel anything but fear and apprehension.

'Something's coming up the hill,' Ellis observed. 'We'll wait until it goes past before we set off.'

Not for anything would Merrin have smiled at this evidence of her employer's caution. He was a nervous passenger and a hopeless driver, but put him in a yacht and he had taken on hurricanes.

'It sounds like a Land Rover,' she said.

It was a Range Rover, an enormous thing which took the steep grade without any loss of speed. Merrin watched as the driver swung the wheel over, the hair at the back of her head lifting. The engine was cut and he jumped down from the vehicle.

It was Blase, and he had been expecting her.

Even as Ellis exclaimed, 'Well, is this a welcoming committee?' and laughed, and shook hands with him, she knew that he had come here for just this reason. To see her before anyone else. To see what six years and disillusionment of the cruellest kind had made of the girl he had seduced and then abandoned.

With the courage of desperation she gave him her hand, lifting her eyes to meet the green-gold blaze of his.

'Well, well, well,' he said softly as his fingers closed on hers with hurtful strength. 'So this is little Merrin Mowatt! Welcome back to Blackrocks, Merrin.'

The words, the tone couldn't be faulted. But his eyes damned her to hell and when he released her hand the tips of her fingers were white where his had crushed them.

Dear kind Ellis stepped into the breach. 'Merrin was just pointing out the station, Blase. Sure you don't mind it being used as a background to murder and mayhem?'

Laughter glinted in the deep eyes. 'Not in the least. What's this one to be about?'

'The drug trade.' Ellis's features settled into a familiar pattern of obstinacy. 'And that's all I'll tell you. I'm always terrified that if I say too much about a plot it will go dry on me.' He took a deep breath. 'You should can this air! I foresee a very happy few weeks. Thank you for asking me up.'

'I hope you won't be too enraptured by your muse to do some socialising,' Blase said smoothly. Tall as Ellis was, his host looked down on him. The years had been kind; he was still broad-shouldered and lean-hipped as a cowboy, but the lines those years had carved into the skin of his face gave him a harsh-featured, cynical look.

'Hell no, it's the least we can do, sing for our supper. I can give a very good imitation of an absentminded genius.'

They smiled at each other, and the little prickles of tension eased, only to be set off again when Blase turned to look at Merrin, asking, 'And what sort of imitations does Merrin give?'

Insolent the words, but not so insolent as the lazy, all-encompassing glance that accompanied them.

'Merrin is the genuine thing,' Ellis returned, frowning, his expression becoming set.

'I wasn't insinuating otherwise. After all, you must remember that we've known her for much longer than you. How long, Merrin?'

'We came here when I was eight.' How composed and cool her voice; she hoped that her face was just as controlled. 'I left two days after my eighteenth birth-day.'

The handsome features showed nothing more than the slightly reminiscent interest of two old acquaint-ances meeting again. 'So it was ten years. And for a couple of those you lived with us at the homestead.' Once more that darting glance, hard, rapier-sharp. 'How long have you lived with Ellis?'

'I've worked for Ellis for—oh, five years.' And make what you like of that, she thought, defiance touching her skin with a fugitive colour. It was totally unfair to involve Ellis in this battle; she had understood only too clearly what the question implied and she resented it, on Ellis's behalf as well as her own.

'We'll have quite a bit of catching up to do,' he said, and behind the smile the threat stood clear. I'm going to enjoy that, he told her without words. Oh, how I'm going to enjoy that!

Ellis frowned again, faintly ill at ease, his shrewd glance moving from one to the other. 'Well, we'd better move on, I suppose. Where are you headed, Blase? I'm quite sure you didn't come this way to meet us.'

'I'm afraid not. I have a little business to see to at a neighbour's, but I'll be home fairly soon. Aunt Hope is eagerly waiting for you; she'll keep you occupied until I get there.'

Again he smiled. Once Merrin had thought he had a beautiful smile; now it held only cynicism spiced with derision. She turned away abruptly, pulses racing as he put her back into the car.

'I'll see you shortly,' he promised after closing the door on her, and then he strode across to the Range Rover, tall and broad and lithe, long legs encased in jeans, hair the colour of dark honey emphasising the proud lines of his head and features.

He lifted his hand in salute before setting his vehicle in motion. The sound of its engine faded. Merrin switched on the key of the Mercedes.

Silence kept them company until they reached the

bottom of the hill. Then Ellis said abruptly, 'I don't know that it was such a good idea to bring you here. He's a hard man to decipher, but it seemed to me that he's still got it in for you.'

'More than likely,' she answered calmly. 'But I think we can manage to keep things cool. We'll be here only a few weeks and he's not going to abuse me in front of the rest of you. And you can be quite sure I'm not going to allow any heart-to-heart conversations. As you pointed out, we're all civilised beings.'

It was impossible to cross her fingers, but she knew an irrational desire to make some sort of propitiatory gesture towards fate. She knew—who better?—that beneath that superbly handsome, magnetic exterior Blase hid some very uncivilised attitudes and reactions. Short though that meeting had been it had revealed that the years had not modified his attitude to her. He still hated her. From being apprehensive about this return to Blackrocks she was now definitely worried. No way was she going to allow herself to be alone with her clearly unwilling host.

'Of course.' Ellis's voice was just a shade dry. 'Well, how did it go?'

Merrin bit her lip. 'I was a bit shattered, but that was all. Honestly, Ellis, I think everything will go much better if you forget that I ever blurted out my dreary little story. I don't want you to feel that you have to defend me; that could well put a strain on your friendship with Blase. After all, what can he do? A few nasty cracks aren't going to hurt me now. If that meeting has done anything it's showed me that whatever I felt for him six years ago has gone. We're two different people.'

'What do you feel for him now?'

She laughed wryly. 'Caution.'

While they spoke they had made their way across low, rolling country towards the coast. Now they rattled over the first of the cattlestops which replaced gates on the road, and incidentally acted as an early warning system to announce the arrival of visitors.

'Well, you probably won't go far wrong if you keep that firmly in mind,' Ellis told her, smiling with something which was very close kin to relief.

The road wound beneath enormous, aged macrocarpa trees, their spiky coniferous branches scenting the drowsy air. Merrin felt an upwelling of the old yearning and quenched it by reflecting on Ellis's relief at her attitude. If necessary he would come to her defence, but he would be infinitely happier if there was no need to!

So, no stupidities, she told herself firmly. After all, what could Blase do? Just hidden insults, a contempt which was so deep that she had felt it beating against her in icy waves: she could cope with that. She was as strong as he, and she would not allow herself to be goaded into any sort of retaliation. If she knew him at all that would really infuriate him.

'The workers' cottages,' she said, pointing out five houses set back from the road.

'Cottages? They look good substantial homes to me.'

A smile touched the soft perfection of her mouth. 'They're always called cottages, a left-over from the days when no one cared much what the hired help lived in, I suppose. Two of those are new since my day.' One had replaced the house where she had lived with her parents, but she saw no reason to mention that.

'Anything else?'

She shrugged. 'I'm watching the road. There's the homestead above us.'

It stood, serenely beautiful, a long low white-painted building about forty years old, designed by an architect who had married the needs of the Stanhopes of those days with the drama and beauty of the land and seascape.

'Superb!' Ellis exclaimed half under his breath.

'Like its owner,' Merrin agreed cynically. 'Inside it's marvellous too. Antiques and magnificent modern fur-

niture, *objets d'art*, paintings—oh, the Stanhopes have superb taste and money enough to indulge it. An invitation to stay at Blackrocks is keenly sought after.'
Her expression became shuttered, almost sombre as she took the car between banks of hibiscus and oleanders towards the house. The drive was an immense circle, the round area in the middle an island of vegetation, jungle-thick, jungle-bright, effectively blocking the front of the house from the gate. 'Royalty has stayed here,' she told Ellis calmly, drawing up outside the panelled front door. 'And quite a few of the better behaved actors and film stars, diplomats and politicians, but no pop stars, of course.'

Ellis laughed, admiring the wide pillared portico, the tubbed hydrangeas massed in lilac and blue profusion, and the air of dreamy grace which lay over the house and garden.

'I'm glad to see that your sense of humour is still intact,' he said, 'even if it does seen to be tinged with cynicism. Ah, who have we here?'

Merrin felt ice stiffen her backbone. With a smile which was as cold and remote as the Antarctic mountains Mrs Grier—Hope Grier, the sister of Blase's father—came through the door.

'Merrin,' she said quietly. 'You don't look a day older, my dear.'

The same could not be said of her. Hair that had been discreetly blonde was now grey; time had dealt harshly with the soft, fine skin, but the features, so like her nephew's, were still as arrogant, still set in complacent lines. Hope Grier looked what she was, a woman who never felt the need to examine her motives or question her actions.

Merrin performed the introductions, watched as Ellis instituted a thawing process, and fell naturally into her old place, two steps behind, as Hope took him into the house.

'You'll want to see your room first,' she said now, 'so Sandy will bring your luggage in. Mr Kimber, I've

given you a room with a view of the sea. And Merrin,'
for the first time a faint unease penetrated Hope's
social mask, 'Blase thought you would probably prefer
your old room. If you don't, we can easily prepare
another.'

So she was to be kept very firmly in her place.
Merrin smiled. 'No, I'm more than happy to have it,
thank you.'

'It's been redecorated.' Hope indicated the passage
which led past the kitchen and necessary offices. 'Do
you remember the way?'

'Vividly.' Almost nothing had changed. The place
even smelt the same, an amalgam of beeswax, the perfume of flowers and the faint, evocative scent of old
furniture with a tang of the sea overlying everything
else.

Someone moved in the kitchen. Resisting the urge
to put her head in through the door and see if it was
still Mrs Fieldgate who reigned there, Merrin went
quietly on down until the passage ended in a door.
And there was her room, originally the servants' sitting
room. It had been pleasant and undistinguished before;
now it was furnished in such luxury that she stood in
the doorway, her wide smooth brow pleated in astonishment, looking around as if to seek something that
remained from the room that once had been hers.

There was nothing. That room had been a comfortable place to sleep, nothing more. This was a kind of
boudoir, a bedroom which had been given over to the
worship of femininity. Gone was her narrow bed; to
take its place there was a wide divan heaped with silken
cushions over a pale cream spread. Silks and satins,
soft colours, furniture in an Eastern style—she flushed
suddenly, pressing hands to her cheeks. This room was
almost decadent, made for the enjoyment of sensual
delights in an exotic, erotic ambience.

She was still standing in the middle of the room
looking around in astonishment when a knock heralded
the entrance of a middle-aged man, tall and thin and

wiry with pale uninterested eyes. He carried her bags in, setting them down with a thump.

'Thank you,' Merrin said softly.

He nodded. 'Bathroom's through that door,' he told her laconically on the way out.

It was tiny, but there again the same voluptuous luxury was evident. As she washed and changed into a plain, almost severe dress Merrin fought down the unease which such opulence gave her. This was a suite for a mistress. Her teeth caught on her bottom lip, then she shrugged. She was a fool to let somebody's whim unnerve her. It took her no more than a few minutes to unpack her bags and put the clothes away, then she reapplied lipstick and surveyed herself in the mirrored doors of the wardrobe.

Small and very slender, she could never be called beautiful, but she knew that flawless skin and the cast of her features gave her an exotic attraction emphasised by eyes of a startling dark green outlined with lashes as black as her hair. Once she had cursed her desirability, but over the years she had developed an air of detachment which was forbidding enough to put most men off. Now it was almost a second skin; she relaxed only with a few close friends. It was they who saw her as she really was, possessed of a quick, somewhat cynical sense of humour and the kind of heart which was too soft for her own good.

'You'll do,' she told her reflection, frowned, then left the beautiful, disturbing room to find Ellis and Hope.

CHAPTER TWO

THEY were out on the terrace, overlooking the sea through a tangle of white, heavily scented mandevillea flowers. Hope Grier looked up as Merrin came through the door and smiled. No warmth reached her eyes.

'Ah, there you are. I was just telling Mr Kimber that it must be six years since you left us.' The cool glance rested a moment on the thin gold wedding ring on Merrin's finger, then slipped upwards to meet her eyes for a moment before moving on to Ellis. 'I suppose you'll notice quite a few changes.'

'The view from the lookout is still much the same,' Merrin responded. It was incredible that this woman, now seemingly absorbed in pouring tea, should have lied, thrown a young girl to the wolves for the sake of her son.

This occasion must be as painful for her as it was for Merrin. The thought struck home; compassion softened the cool green depths of Merrin's eyes. When Hope spoke to her again she replied with more composure so that when Blase joined them after half an hour or so they seemed completely at ease together.

His arrival brought tension, a vivid awareness which set at nought the restful atmosphere of the garden. Merrin's nerves tautened; meeting the hard hazel glance was like forcing oneself into an icy sea. She managed it by summoning up every ounce of resolution she possessed, determined not to let him see how intimidating she found him.

However, she was extremely glad when, after tea had been drunk, he bore Ellis off to his office.

'Where they'll swap school stories and catch up with old friends,' Hope said pleasantly. 'I'm sure you'd like a rest, Merrin, you've driven a long way today. Or perhaps a walk in the garden?'

Obviously here was another person who wanted no tête-à-têtes.

'Yes, I'd like to renew my acquaintance with the garden,' Merrin replied.

From now on it would be easier, for Ellis was eager to get going, so she would be busy—and out of the way—all day. Which left only the evenings, and she was quite sure she could avoid Hope and Blase for much of the time then.

But in the meantime it was good to stroll across the wide lawns which led down to the pool. In the scented, shaded ambience of the garden she even managed to forget for a while the threat to her peace of mind represented by this visit. The disciplined mask which usually hid her emotions relaxed as she made her way slowly past beds where flowers and shrubs enhanced each other's beauty in the tangle of form and colour which, although semi-tropical in luxuriance, fitted in perfectly with the restrained grace of the house.

There had, however, been extensive re-landscaping since she had lived here. Keenly interested, she wandered slowly and without purpose to arrive at the pool. It lay at the farthest extent of the gardens where the shrubbery eased into a plantation of trees sheltering the area from the west and the south. Once there had been a marshy area at the foot of a slope; many years ago it had been drained and the pool built, a formal rectangle lined with mosaic tiles, Roman in style, elegant but out of place in this wide landscape of sea and sky.

Now it was much larger, irregular in shape, set amidst gardens which had been carefully planted to look informal beneath trees and the slender lacy beauty of silver ferns, their black, rough trunks a splendid contrast to the soft lime green fronds backed with silver. The mosaic tiles were gone; instead the interior of the pool had been painted so that the water was as dark as a pond in the bush. The whole area had been skilfully planned to look like a forest clearing with the expanse of water as its focal point.

Merrin's eyes were drawn across the dark slate of the terrace to where once a fake Greek temple had stood. It was gone too, replaced by a long low building of stained wood built into the hillside. Loungers and chairs tempted; Merrin walked across and sat down, staring into the water. If she closed her eyes she could still see that little temple, so out of place, so calmly elegant, with its columns and the room behind them, cool even in the height of summer.

It had been February, the hottest month, and she had continued her habit of coming down very early in the morning to swim. Often Blase had guests over in the evening and she did not like to swim then; he was always the same, like a big brother, but sensitive as ever, Merrin knew that Hope preferred her to stay out of sight. And she did not like to see the efforts some of the women made to attract Blase's attention. Nor did she enjoy Terry Grier's quips and the way his eyes ran over her body. She would be glad when the holidays finished and he went back to varsity.

So she used to rise with the sun and slip across the dew wet grass to embrace the cool water with all the enthusiasm of her seventeen years. She had assumed that no one else knew of her early morning swims, so Blase's appearance had surprised her—and thrilled her.

For almost as long as she could remember she had loved him, and every time she saw him her heart beat faster beneath her slight breasts.

But that cool gold and blue morning she had said nothing, just smiled at him, then continued her lengths, practising her strokes with the methodical determination which marked her character.

When she finished he grinned at her. 'Let's see if you can beat me now.'

It was an old joke, as was the fact that he gave her several yards start and still won easily. But this time when she stretched out her hand to grab the side of the pool it was his chest she touched. Embarrassed and rather frightened by her reactions, she pulled her hand away, but he said harshly, 'No,' and held it there, sliding her fingers over the firm wet skin to tangle with the mat of hair above his heart.

Something moved in her stomach. She lifted the wet spikes of her lashes and looked at him, noting that although he looked stern there was a glint deep in his hazel eyes which she had never seen before.

'Blase?' The word was tentative, half whispered, and he smiled, his other hand moving to clasp her shoulder and bring her towards him.

She wore a skimpy, very aged bikini. When they touched she felt the imprint of his entire body against her. She should have been frightened, but it seemed entirely natural to be held in his arms, entirely natural to feel his mouth on her forehead and know that whatever he felt for her was far from brotherly.

'Hush,' he said, and kissed her eyes shut and covered her mouth with his.

Merrin stiffened but his lips were softly coaxing, tender and yet persistent. There had been no one else for her, so she was completely innocent, but some instinct made her relax, opening her mouth in an invitation as sensual as it was shy.

Blase laughed, a curious breathy sound, while his body hardened against hers and she knew what he wanted. For a moment she was frightened, pulling away, but he said softly, 'I won't hurt you, Merrin, I promise. I've waited so long for you to grow up that I've just run out of patience. I love you, honey girl, and I know you love me.'

Before she could say anything he accepted the invitation her lips proffered, plundering her mouth in a kiss as far removed from the few he had given her until then as the kitchen cat was from a lion. Until then she had not known that a kiss could set every nerve jangling into vibrant life, or that her body had needs of its own which overrode completely the promptings of common sense.

When he lifted his head he was trembling, and she felt a wicked triumph that she could so affect him.

'Merrin?' he said softly, framing her face in his lean strong hands.

She was so shy that she couldn't look him in the face. That treacherous instinct drove her to slide her arms across his shoulders and clasp them together behind his neck. She pressed her face into his neck, feeling the strong, quick beat of his heart against her skin. Like this, wet and so close together, they could have been naked. She had no intention of stopping him from whatever he planned to do, so it was with a distinct disappointment that she realised he was climbing up the steps with her in his arms.

When they reached the little temple he lowered her to her feet and looked into her face, his eyes fierce and hot as they swept over the heightened colour in her cheeks and the soft, sweet mouth, slightly bruised from his kiss.

'Oh God,' he groaned, 'I should be hanged! You're only a baby.' And he went to put her from him.

By now she was in the grip of desire far stronger than her fears and shyness. With a boldness she hadn't known she possessed she stood on tiptoe and kissed his shoulder, touching the firm cool skin with her hands and her mouth; she did not realise just how provocative the soft warm fugitive movements were.

'Cut it out!' He grabbed her by her wet hair, but she laughed, for the first time conscious of the power that her femininity gave her and showing it in what must have been a taunting, tempting glance upwards from beneath her lashes.

Beneath her fingertips she felt his heart begin to race. Aloud he said on a soft, thick note, 'Don't tell me you've been hiding a wanton under that schoolgirl façade, honey girl.'

She had wanted to tell him that only he affected her

like that, but he had kissed her again, his hand sliding
across her back to the tie of her bikini, and then it was
too late.

Merrin bit her lip until the blood came. Blase had
accepted her invitation that morning, taking her on one
of the loungers, and when at last they lay in the peace
of satisfied passion the rising sun had striped them like
tigers as it shone between the pillars of the little temple.
If she closed her eyes she could recall it all, the relaxed
langour of their entwined bodies, the sun and the blue
sky, the sounds of the thrush from the top of the magnolia tree, the feel and scent of Blase's body heavy
against hers.

Oh, but she had been so incredibly naïve! Perhaps
losing her mother when she was fifteen had had
something to do with it; she certainly had had no help
from Hope and the only other women who might have
helped her understand the needs of her maturing body
was Moira Fieldgate, the housekeeper. But Moira had
been horrified at a question arising from a biology
lesson Merrin had asked her in all innocence, so after
that there had been no further attempts to confide in
her.

Oh, she had known the facts of life, she thought now
cynically. What she hadn't understood was that hot
blood and proximity could create a situation when
desire was easily mistaken for love. Blase had an immensely magnetic presence and she had fallen victim
to his spell so young that she could not even think of
denying him. When he told her that he loved her she
had accepted him as her master, unable to resist the
promptings of her body and his physical magic.

She had given him the ruling of her life, but he must
have thought that her swift, complete surrender meant
that she was something of the wanton he had called
her, for if he had thought otherwise he would never
have believed Terry's lies.

A bitter smile touched her lips. Had she been more
calculating, had she made him wait for his pleasure, he

might have discounted Terry's poison; her mistake had been her ardour and her generosity.

A morality fable for young girls! Well, she was over it now. But she sat in the westering sunlight with tears on her lashes until a soft movement brought her to her feet, hands clenched at her sides. Blase, of course, his expression hard and dangerous as he came up to her; conscious that to wipe her wet lashes would be to attract the attention she didn't want she turned her head, blinking ferociously. She would *not* show fear.

After a moment she said, 'Hi. What have you done with Ellis?'

'He's busy arranging the office for you.' A long pause before he asked calmly, 'Is he your lover?'

She felt like slapping his insolent face but prudence dictated a wiser course. He was watching her with a cold arrogance as though it would give him great pleasure to retaliate in kind.

'That's no business of yours,' she said distantly, and set off past him to the path which led up to the house.

His hand on her arm was brutal. 'Tell me, damn you!'

It was useless to struggle. One glance at the implacable cast of his features showed her that he had no intention of freeing her until she had given him an answer.

'Why don't you watch us and see?' she taunted. 'And let me go! I hate your touch!'

He smiled and increased the pressure of his fingers until she gasped, white about the mouth.

'Blase . . .' she choked, afraid now as she had been only once before. 'Please – *oh!*'

For he released her, only to run his hand up her arm and across her shoulder, the long strong fingers which had once stroked her flesh into painful excitement now clasping her throat as if he would like to choke her to death.

'Why did you come back, Merrin?' he asked, his glance very cold and hard, that moment of white-hot emotion gone now.

'Ellis needs me.' She was mesmerised by his eyes, unable to look away, unable to lie.

The pressure on her windpipe increased slightly. 'And do you do everything Ellis wants?'

It hurt to swallow, but she did. 'Don't be so offensive! He employs me to type his books for him.'

'Does he know that we were lovers?' Those cruel fingers tightened at her silence. 'I want the truth.'

'Yes.' She took a deep breath, found that she could breathe easily again. His hand dropped to his side. At once she turned, but he caught her by the shoulder and she froze.

'Don't go. We have a lot to discuss. Come and have a drink with me.'

'No. I don't want to talk to you.' Impulsively, knowing before she began that her plea was doomed to failure, she asked, 'Blase, why can't you forget about the past? It's over and done with now; what happened six years ago happened to two entirely different people. Must we carry on old grudges?'

'Why did you tell Ellis of our relationship?'

The same slightly bored voice, the same watchful aura.

Merrin sighed. 'I had to explain why I didn't want to come here.'

'So in spite of your eloquent appeal, you haven't forgotten the past, either.'

'I—no.' She lifted her lashes, looked directly at him. 'I didn't say I had, just that it was time for it to be forgotten. Six years is a long time.'

'I couldn't agree more.' He smiled, the irony almost hidden but not quite. Outwardly the years hadn't altered him much. He had always been inordinately good-looking and still was, but the recklessness of youth had been replaced by an iron self-command which made him forbidding as his younger self had not been.

'See any difference?'

The question made her conscious of her open stare. A faint flush touched her cheeks, but she had enough composure to say calmly, 'Not much. You were a handsome young man—you'll still be good-looking when you hit eighty.'

'And that was all that interested you, wasn't it?' Ignoring her questioning look, he lifted his hand to run his forefinger across her jawline, finishing at the corner of her mouth. 'You've improved. You were a pretty child when you left here; you're beautiful now. They've been profitable years, I gather.'

Merrin thought of Paul, blood across his face from the wound in his head, the baby daughter who had died unborn, the anguish and grief and bitter regret. A stifled sob brought the muscles in her throat into play.

'Very profitable,' she said, stepping back from beneath his hand. 'As you see.'

'There was, of course, your marriage. What happened there? A divorce?'

Thinly she returned, 'No. He died in a car accident,' and looked at him with cold resentment.

'I'm sorry.' He spoke with a carelessness which revealed that she was telling him nothing he had not known before.

Anger at his callous dismissal made her say crisply, 'One gets over anything in time. Which,' she pointed out with determination, 'brings us back to where we started. I don't want to spend my time here avoiding you.'

'Do you think you might?'

'You have ways of making your displeasure felt,' she returned with grim emphasis, pushing back a tendril of hair from her temple.

It was hot, almost sultry, a steamy end to a perfect day. Northland weather, she thought. In this secluded hollow they were sheltered from the breeze which came from the sea each evening as the sun went down behind Blackrock hills. Across her back her dress clung damply, emphasising the slender lines of her body; she could feel drops of perspiration gathering across her nose.

'So we sign a truce, do we?'

She looked up, met the cool, still depths of his eyes. An odd little frisson quivered across her nerves. To banish it, she said swiftly, 'Can't we—after six years?'

Blase held out his hand; after a moment's hesitation she put hers within it, thinking he wished to shake on his decision. But he lifted her hand to his mouth and kissed her fingers before touching his tongue to the palm of it.

Merrin flinched, startled and shocked at the violence of her own reaction. 'What was that in aid of?' she asked, steadying her voice with a considerable amount of effort.

Mockery glinted in his smile. 'An experiment,' he told her as he released her hand. 'So—let's make our bargain. I'll treat you like an old friend and in return you'll behave like one. No more avoiding me as if I had plague, no imitation of an icicle.'

'Just old friends,' she said without emphasis, surprised at his decision but welcoming it.

He smiled, and dropped an arm across her shoulder, turning her so that she faced the steps up to the lawn. As they moved towards them he asked, 'How do you enjoy working for Ellis?'

'Very much. He's a darling and he's very professional—he doesn't throw tantrums or pull rank.'

Her voice softened into affection. She could never forget that when she had applied for the position, frightened and despairing, only two months after the double tragedy of the loss of her child and Paul's death, Ellis had hired her and put up with her amateurish efforts until she developed the skills she now possessed. She owed him so much, perhaps even her sanity.

'Lucky Ellis,' he commented lightly.

'Lucky me.' There could be no mistaking her sincerity. She wanted to make it quite clear that she had absolutely no interest in resuming their affair. That age-old instinct which belongs to all women warned her that although he still despised her he was not immune to her. And she had already been burned in that fire. So if he read rather more into her affection for Ellis than was there she did not mind.

They reached the steps; Merrin used them as an excuse to slip free from the weight of his arm. Six years ago such a casual gesture would have put her into heaven, for then he had insisted on circumspection, never touching her if there was any chance of being seen. What a hypocrite he had been, she thought coldly. Acting like a big brother during the day, friendly but a little distant, while at night . . .

Horrified by the direction of her thoughts, she made some comment about the alterations she had noticed.

He allowed her her freedom, following her lead with an easy charm which was belied by the speculative glint from beneath his lowered lashes. To Ellis, waiting with Hope on the terrace, they must have seemed no more than old lovers who had decided to be friends. At the bottom of the steps to the house Blase said something which made her laugh, the sound clear on the sultry air. Merrin caught Ellis's eye and smiled with all of the reassurance she could muster.

Hope had been watching them too, her patrician features held firmly in control. As if Merrin's laughter eased some tension within her she relaxed into graciousness.

'You were gone so long I thought of sending out a search party,' she remarked, the tone of her voice revealing that she wasn't to be taken seriously.

'I found her admiring the pool.' Blase picked up a decanter. 'I suppose you drink now, Merrin. What can I give you?'

'Sherry, please. Dry.'

It was pleasantly crisp against her tongue, the small ritual of sipping it relaxing her so that she realised just how great a strain the preceding half hour had been.

Suddenly the weeks that Ellis planned to spend on the station seemed like an eternity.

Shivering, she made a remark about the alterations to the garden, directing her thoughts away from her memories. Hope had always been far more interested in the garden than in the house, but her tastes had been set in the formal symmetry of the gardens of her youth. Listening to her as she spoke, Merrin gathered that while she took credit for many of the changes she disapproved of what had been done to the pool.

So it must have been Blase's decision. She wondered why he had made such a clean sweep of what had been an enchanting little folly. She had loved the pool; it had been beautiful, surrounded by the urns brought back by Blase's grandmother from Italy. Filled with camellias and roses and lilies, they had given the place a continental look, formal and restful. The little temple had been decorated to follow suit, with chaise longues and wrought iron furniture. Out of place, of course, a charming old-world folly in a landscape of raw primitive power; the forest pool was much more in keeping with Blackrocks.

Just another change, like her redecorated bedroom and the new houses. Six years was a long time and Blase was a progressive landowner; there would be other changes all of them for the better.

'. . . so when the old bushes died, we planted the latest Hawaiian ones in their place,' Hope finished. 'They do very well here.'

Guiltily Merrin nodded, the sun warm across the soft waves on her black head. 'Do you still collect old roses?' she asked.

It was pleasant to sit in this sheltered spot and drink good sherry while the sun went down. From this angle the sea was hidden from view, the only evidence of its presence the gentle hush of the waves on the ocean beach. Built especially to scoop up the evening sun, the terrace was bordered with honey-scented allysum, its crystal white flowers decorated with tiny blue-grey

moths. Oleanders bloomed, silken petals contrasting
with long blue fronds of rosemary. Among the shrubs
an orange tree flowered, the waxy white blossoms
heavily, erotically sweet-scented on the bland air.

Life among the very rich, Merrin thought sar-
donically, making appropriate noises as Hope talked on.
Behind them Ellis and Blase chatted, their friendship
revealed by the long silences which punctuated their
conversation. It should have been an idyllic hour
before dinner, a time of relaxation and good companionship, especially as Blase appeared to have ac-
quiesced to her plea.

So why was she uneasy? Perhaps because she
couldn't quite believe it. Blase had agreed too quickly
to her request. It would have been far more in character for him to have carried on his vendetta to a bitter,
inevitable conclusion. He had been hurt in his most
vulnerable place, his sexual pride; his cruelty during
that last week had revealed that. Had he loved her, had
there been any other emotion there besides desire, he
would at least have given her a chance to explain what
had happened. But he had refused to listen, stopping
her with hard, contemptuous kisses and once with his
hand, using words and her subjugation as his weapons,
until she had been shattered and so demoralised that
her flight from Blackrocks was necessary for her
sanity.

Dusk crept across the hills, a blue veil beneath the
green and pink evening sky, bringing with it a melancholy which made Merrin shiver. She had been so
young, a child at the mercy of needs she was too immature to handle. Like a child she had given her heart
completely and like a child she had fled its brutal re-
pudiation, hiding herself away to lick her wounds. Only
it hadn't been possible, for childish as she had been
her body had betrayed her and she had married Paul
to give Blase's baby a home and a father. Her unwit-
ting selfishness had killed the child and driven her
husband to his death.

Unwillingly her eyes moved, focused on Blase's profile. A glass loosely clasped in his fingers, he was leaning against one of the columns which supported the roof, staring across his heritage of green acres.

Against the feathery foliage of a jacaranda tree his features were strongly outlined, the harsh bone structure unsoftened by any slackness. The arrogant line of jaw and nose revealed uncompromising strength, a man who wielded power over himself and others.

It seemed incredible that she had carried his child for six months until . . . But she would not allow herself any further maudlin remembrances. The last of her sherry slid, smooth and dry, down her throat and immediately he moved, turning towards her.

'More, Merrin?'

Had he been watching her, keeping her in his vision even though he seemed so withdrawn? Merrin's fingers tightened around her glass. After a moment she forced them to relax, answering in a colourless voice, 'No, thank you.'

From behind came Ellis's comment, teasing and affectionate. 'She had no head for alcohol, I've discovered.'

'Sensible girl. Hope? No? Shall we go in? It's inclined to get chilly as soon as the sun sets.'

A note in the deep tones caught Merrin's attention. She looked up, met his eyes and turned her head away sharply at the glinting, smiling mockery in his glance. So he had noticed that involuntary shudder. He had been watching her, assessing her reactions, probing for weaknesses, his watchfulness an intrusion on her privacy. Feeling as though he had stripped her, she followed Hope into the house.

After dinner he took her and Ellis down to the room he had set aside for them, and stood while she looked around, her green eyes carefully blank in the careful blankness of her expression. Not for anything would she let him see that she hated the thought of working in this room.

'Very nice,' she said tonelessly, and smiled at Ellis. 'Feel the juices starting to run?'

'Oh, yes.' He smiled back, warm, friendly, immensely familiar and dear. 'So enjoy tonight, Merrin. From now on you work, and I mean *work*. Like a galley-slave, in fact. Incidentally, did you get that letter away to the publisher before we left?'

'Why, yes. I posted it yesterday.'

He frowned. 'Pity. I'd intended ... oh, well, leave it.'

Merrin could feel Blase's presence in the room, the crackling tension that warned her when he was within her personal area of safety. With a mental shrug she ignored it, saying, 'No, if you want to get another one off to him I'll do it.' Deliberately she swung around, looked with calm enquiry at Blase. 'Does the mail still go on Tuesdays and Thursdays, Blase?'

'It does.'

Turning back to Ellis, she said, 'Tell me what you want to say and I'll do it in time to catch the mail.'

From the door came Blase's voice, deep and cool. 'I'll leave you to it. Come and share a drink with me before you go to bed, Ellis.'

As soon as he had closed the door behind him Ellis said quietly, 'I gather you've made up your differences?'

'Agreed to forget them, anyway.' She moved across to the table where the typewriter sat, opened a drawer and pulled out a scratchpad and pen. 'O.K., what do you want to say to Mr Cummings?'

Accepting her decision to say no more on that subject, Ellis began to dictate. Five minutes later he left her, no doubt to enjoy that nightcap with his host.

When she had finished Merrin found herself sitting at the desk, hands loosely clasped in her lap as she looked around the room. It was a kind of annexe to Blase's office, and when she had lived here it had been her domain. Then it had been a cosy Victorian room panelled with dark wood, a dark red carpet on the floor and crimson drapes at the windows.

It, too, had been redecorated. The walls were covered in grasscloth the same pale straw colour as the background of the Chinese rug on the floor. Across the windows velvet curtains picked up the exact shade of blue in the pattern on the rug, and the heavy glassed bookcases had been replaced by lighter, modern shelves above a sleek built-in cabinet. On the wall was a Japanese embroidery, a spare, stark thing in blue and beige of a woman in a kimono.

It was an airy, sophisticated room, about as big a contrast to its previous self as anything could be. A decorator must have done it. It certainly wasn't Hope's style.

On an impulse Merrin tried one of the doors of the cabinet, found the shelves stacked with the paraphernalia of any office. Guiltily she closed it up, and turned, and there was Blase just inside the door, watching her.

'You gave me a fright!' she exclaimed jumpily.

'Sorry.' He wasn't, of course. But he came farther in, and smiled, very big in his dark slacks and white shirt. 'Have you everything you need?'

Her breath caught in her throat. He loomed, she thought fancifully, too big and too dominating in the room. 'Yes, thank you.'

Those hazel eyes were almost abstracted as they roved the contours of her face. Always he had possessed the ability to hide his thoughts behind a mask, subduing even the leaping, glinting lights in his eyes so that no one knew what went on in that clever, tough brain.

'Do you like your bedroom?' he asked with casual interest.

She nodded, strangely uneasy and hating herself for her lack of poise. 'Who wouldn't? It's beautiful.' Something impelled her to add, 'You've had a lot of redecorating done.'

'Not much. Several rooms which needed it. The

records from here have been stored on microfilm and are in one of the rooms at the back of the house.' He grinned suddenly, and she was drawn back into the perilous orbit of his charm. 'It was that or get rid of them; you must remember how much stuff we had, right from the time old Matt Stanhope bought Blackrocks. We had a hellish time classifying everything. One of my cousins is a librarian and she spent her holidays doing it. I'll show you, if you like.'

The years seemed to fade into a distant limbo, forgotten. Relaxed for the first time since Ellis had dropped his bombshell, Merrin responded, 'I'd like to, but not tonight.' A yawn approached; she covered her mouth and said after it had gone, 'I'm tired. Ellis is so jittery in the car he makes me tense when I drive.'

'Then you must go to bed, but before you do, come and see the computer.'

'Computer?'

Laughing at her astonishment, he took her by the elbow and led her into the study next door. 'Behold,' he said, indicating a neat computer terminal which sat on a desk top.

'Good heavens!' Merrin was awed, approaching it as if it might suddenly talk to her. 'But, Blase, what on earth do you use it for?'

'Think.'

She screwed up her nose at him, suddenly metamorphosed back to the schoolgirl who had been completely at home here. 'It's memory would come in awfully handy—you could store all the information you have about your flock and the cattle too.'

'Got it in one. It holds all the data I need for my stock improvement scheme. There are ten of us who pool the genetic resources of our flocks. Eventually we hope to breed easy-care, high-producing sheep. We can get a print-out any time on any aspect of any animal's performance. The same applies to the cattle.'

'Not just that, either,' she said shrewdly. 'Is this hooked in with your other properties?'

He nodded. 'Yes. I don't have to tell you just how much paper work and checking back there used to be. With the best will in the world there were occasions when mistakes were made simply because we couldn't lay our hands on the information quickly enough. This way I've all the data here to help me make decisions. It's saved me a hell of a lot of time.'

Merrin looked around, her expression absorbed. Nothing had changed in this room, or very little, certainly not the wholesale clearing out that had happened in her bedroom and office. An idea fretted at the edge of her consciousness and was gone, but her uneasiness returned.

To cover it she asked briskly, 'Is it hard to work?'

'No. Any averagely intelligent person can use it. Do you remember Erana Williamson, the wife of one of the shepherds? She has no difficulty.'

'Does she do all the office work now?'

A conventional enough question, so why did she turn away so that he couldn't see her face as she asked it?

And there was an odd note in his voice when he answered. 'Yes. She comes up each morning. Her children are all at school now, of course.'

Merrin nodded. Erana's family had been toddlers when she left. 'Is Mrs Fieldgate still here?' she asked obliquely.

'She's still here. Wally died—oh, three years ago. A chap called Sandy Davies is our cowman now.'

'I think he brought my bags in.' She did not tell him that she had been relieved not to see Wally Fieldgate. Six years ago he and his wife had made it quite clear that they sided with the family, so much so that they had flatly refused to help her leave the station, had even told Blase of her pleas for aid. A cold shiver touched her skin as she remembered the scene which had followed.

Incredible that she should be standing here in this room only a few feet away, talking so calmly to him!

The last time she had been here he had only just managed to prevent himself from hitting her. Balked of any physical expression of his savage anger, he had used his tongue instead, lashing her with insults which had reduced her to a shivering, hopeless wreck.

Never again, she thought, repeating a vow she had made after Paul's death. Never again would she be a helpless victim, pushed around by forces stronger than she was. From now on she would be in control.

It had worked, too. And would continue to do so unless she allowed anyone to steal that control from her. Blase was strong, ruthless in his use of power, but he no longer had any dominion over her, for she was as self-sufficient as he, equally strong.

'That's a very challenging look,' he observed softly, reaching out a hand to touch a soft curl which had fallen across her temple.

Almost she flinched, but apart from a swift indrawn breath she managed to hide her reaction. 'Just thinking,' she said coolly as she moved away.

'Remembering?'

The dark hair swirled as she shook her head. 'No,' she lied, infusing her voice with rueful amusement. 'Memories can be a nuisance. I only remember happy things.'

'And your life here was not happy?'

It could have been any idle question but she knew now that he was playing with her, had been all evening. Well, what else could she expect? It was stupid to carry on a vendetta, but he was not the type to forget and forgive so easily.

Telling herself very firmly that he could no longer hurt her, Merrin returned, 'Some of it was very happy, some not in the least.' She faked a yawn, allowed her eyes to meet his. 'And now I really must go to bed, or I'll be exhausted tomorrow. Goodnight, Blase.'

Smiling, her expression as bland and uncommunicative as his, she walked past him. She felt his gaze on her until she was through the door; it took

all her self-control not to run the last few steps. And I
hope you fry! she thought savagely as she made her
way to the little room where Hope would be watching
television.

Ten minutes later she was in the sanctuary of her
own room, watching through the open French
windows as an enormous full moon came smokily up
from the sea. The tears came then—the last tears, she
vowed, that she would ever shed for a dream of love
lost and betrayed.

The crying jag left her with a headache. She took an
aspirin with a glass of water and after removing her
make-up lay back on the bed for some minutes with
cotton wool pads soaked in cold water over her eyes.
The last thing she wanted to parade before Blase
Stanhope's altogether too-perceptive gaze was eyes
reddened from weeping.

Although it was officially autumn the nights were
still summer warm. Merrin woke with a slight start to
find moonlight spilling across her floor in a sheet of
silver. A glance at her watch showed that it was only
between midnight and one, but she felt that she had
slept for hours.

After twenty minutes or so spent tossing and turning
she got up, pulled on jeans and a shirt, slipped her feet
into thongs and went out of the French windows, down
through the exotic scents and shapes of the garden to a
small gate set between two enormous old magnolia
trees. Everything was as still as a painting, an ex-
travaganza of blacks and silver, with the half moon slab
of the sea pale against the paler sky where the autumn
stars turned in their slow immutable paths.

The path wound its way across a paddock and then
down between flax bushes towards the sea. Not a dog
barked, not a sheep bleated, but in the waters of the
lagoon a fish jumped, silver against deeper silver.
Mullet coming up with the tide, she decided.

Swiftly she ran through the tough, coarse grasses
which covered the low sandhills, preventing them from

encroaching on to the land. Within her a fey sensation burgeoned wild as the night and her mood, until she was gripped by an intolerable anticipation which had to be exorcised by action. It took only a moment to strip off her clothes; she waded into the milk-warm waters of the lagoon and as silently as any other dweller in the sea struck out across the smooth expanse. It made sense to avoid the channel where the tide would be sweeping in, but the lagoon was so large there was plenty of space to exercise away her restlessness.

When at last she thought she might be tired enough to sleep again she walked gracefully up on to the sand, running her fingers through her hair and shaking it loose with a fluid graceful movement.

Then the horse under the gnarled old pohutukawa lifted a hoof, whickered softly. Merrin froze, her hands protecting her modesty in the age-old feminine gesture.

'Too late,' Blase taunted as he swung himself down from the horse and came towards her, dark as the shadows in his dark clothes, his hair gleaming silver in the moonlight.

Merrin stared, her eyes dilating. Oh, but he was big and he was smiling. He was every woman's nightmare of the booted ravisher in the darkness! And now, when she needed them most, her wits, her very reactions seemed to have deserted her so that as he came up to her she could only stand there, frozen as a statue.

'What are you doing here?' she asked in a voice no louder than a whisper.

'Like you, I couldn't sleep.' He stopped in front of her, hands on hips, and looked down, his eyes roving the glistening curves and planes of her body with deliberate insolence. 'But I use up my excess energy by riding.'

Anger at his disregard of all the courtesies brought life back into her frozen limbs, swamping her embar-

rassment in a flood of hot emotion. But she reined it
in hard. Instinct told her that she was in great danger;
common sense told her that to run or reveal her true
reactions could well be disastrous.

So she said calmly, 'Well, you scared hell out of me.
Have you been there all the time?'

'Yes.' He reached out, wound a damp curl around
his forefinger and said, 'You know, you're more
beautiful now than you were six years ago.' His hand
cupped the back of her neck as he pulled her towards
him. 'More beautiful, and infinitely more desirable,'
he said thickly.

Merrin put both her hands on his chest, not pushing
but obviously determined. 'No,' she said, quite calmly.
'No, Blase. I don't want to make love with you.'

'No?' His eyes were laughing coldly at her from
beneath his heavy eyelids, his mouth twisted into a
smile. 'Why not?'

'I don't have to explain why,' she told him, adding
swiftly, 'But if you must know, it's because I don't
fancy you.'

'Then I'll just have to make you, won't I?' he said,
and kissed her.

Not on the mouth. No, his lips closed her eyes first,
and then moved, oh, so slowly, down to where a pulse
throbbed heavily against the wet skin of her throat.
Merrin felt the heat of his desire beat against her as if
the door of a furnace had been opened.

When she shivered he said against her skin, 'I knew
how to warm you.'

'I don't want you,' she said clearly, coldly. Her anger
had been subdued, controlled by her will to become a
weapon. No doubt he thought that all it needed was a
little caressing and she would once again be a willing
slave to his desire. Later, she knew, she would feel
humiliation, but at this moment she was icily furious.

'Don't you?' He lifted his head and looked down
into her rigid face, and the desire she so feared was
gone, so that all that she saw in his expression was

speculation, cool and assessing. 'I think you're lying. Or perhaps you've forgotten . . .'

And still he didn't kiss her. Instead, as he watched her from beneath his lashes his hands moved slowly, smoothly across her gleaming skin, touching, caressing, until one reached the mound of her breast. She drew a deep breath as his fingers found the sensitive peak there, almost bit her lip at the betraying kick of desire in her loins.

'No,' he murmured softly, 'you haven't forgotten, Merrin. Remember how good we were together? Do you still make those funny little noises in your throat?' And when she refused to answer he smiled and continued, 'Shall I find out?'

As he spoke his hand had run slowly, intimately down her spine, holding her against him so that she could feel the hunger in him.

'No,' she said defiantly, lifting her head. The heavy clinging waves swirled around her small, pale face. 'Leave it, Blase, for heaven's sake. I'm not interested in raking over old embers, and I'm surprised that you are.' Sudden bitterness sharpened her voice. 'You might find it amusing but I'm afraid I can't forget that last week I spent here so easily. You hated the thought that I had another lover. Well, there've been more since then.'

The tormenting, teasing fingers stilled their stroking. In the moonlight his expression was shuttered, any thoughts and emotions hidden behind the beautiful mask of his features. Merrin's eyes searched his face, moving from broad brow to high cheekbones, the strongly sculptured framework beneath the tanned skin. Most handsome men lived only through their looks, but when one saw Blase it was strength and determination which impinged, not the fact that he was handsome.

'Naturally,' he said quietly, and let her go. As she turned he added with a soft purposefulness which raised the hair on the back of her neck, 'But I intend to take advantage of the situation, so be warned.'

'Do you mind?' she asked frigidly.

He laughed. 'Not in the least. You look like Undine rising from the water, soulless but lovely enough to make a man lose his soul. And no, I'm not going to turn away. I've seen you dress often enough before.'

'*Must* you keep harking back?' Angered, she jerked her clothes on over her wet skin, aware of his gaze on the slender pallor of her body. He was enjoying her humiliation; she yanked her tee-shirt over her head, ignoring him as best she could, but it was impossible. He was too big, too dangerous with his aggressive masculinity held so strongly in check, and she hated him because for one moment he had made her feel the fluid clutch of desire within her.

'You can come up behind me,' he said when she was dressed.

She shook her head. 'I'll walk.'

'And wake everyone up?'

Reluctantly she looked up at him. 'How come?'

'The dogs.'

'Oh.' Yes, she remembered the dogs. 'They'll hear you coming too.'

'They're used to me.' As if bored with her cavilling he grabbed her wrist and urged her across to where the horse waited, 'Come on.'

It was not the first time that she had ridden behind him, but she was going to make sure that it was the last. He had bridled his big gelding, but as she had always done he had ridden it bareback.

After a few minutes during which she held herself away from him, her hands gripping his belt at the side he said over his shoulder, 'I won't infect you, Merrin, so stop being so bloody stupid. Put your arms around me properly.'

Biting her lip, she did as she was told, linking her hands around him, her head turned sideways against the hard muscles of his back. And that treacherous pleasure in the physical perfection of the man heated her cheeks, making the blood run faster and thinner through every vein in her body. Fervently she hoped that he could not feel the acceleration in her pulse, because his heart beat steadily and without any increase in force against her hands.

He let her off at the little gate, waiting until she was almost through it before saying softly, 'Merrin.'

'Yes?'

'I meant what I said about taking advantage of your being here. Should I tell Ellis?'

She would not look at him, but her skin knew that he was watching her, a darker silhouette against the dark cliff called Blackrocks.

'Why should you?' she asked bitterly. 'You've never denied yourself where I am concerned.'

The moon caught a flash of white as he smiled. 'You've developed a mighty chip on your shoulder,' he jeered. 'I don't remember you ever saying no. Goodnight.'

CHAPTER THREE

THE breakfast room was small and warm, placed so that it scooped up every ray of the morning sun. Merrin was terrified that because of her midnight expedition she might be late up, but her internal clock woke her at seven o'clock as usual. By half past she was sitting at the table, spooning passsionfruit pulp over half a chilled rock-melon.

Almost immediately Ellis followed her in, newly-shaven and morose. Aware that it took at least two cups of tea before he woke up, Merrin poured the first and handed it to him.

'Thank you,' he said glumly, stirring it with a complete lack of interest.

Normally he read the newspaper over his solitary breakfast, but of course the daily paper didn't arrive here until mid-afternoon. So he frowned at the table-cloth, for the moment completely uninterested in the sparkling, glittering world through the window.

However the ripe, musky scent of the rock-melon must have impinged. After five minutes he said, 'You'd think they'd produce a melon without that disgusting perfume.'

'You would,' Merrin agreed, her mouth twitching.

He grinned. 'You're a darling. Why don't I marry you?'

'It's because she's not married to you that she's a darling.' Blase's voice was coolly ironic as he came in through the French window. 'If you married her she would immediately expect you to converse with witty charm over the breakfast table every morning. Security has a deleterious effect on manners.'

He was carrying a cup of coffee and looked and sounded cynically pleased with himself. The hazel eyes lingered on Merrin's averted profile with open admiration. 'Mind you, it might be worth it,' he finished, the sardonic tone of his voice contradicting his words.

Ellis managed a smile. 'I'd forgotten how revoltingly smug you are at the crack of dawn,' he complained. 'Merrin at least has the decency not to flaunt her good humour at me. Why don't you go and shear a sheep or something?'

'Today I take you around Blackrocks,' Blase told him. 'You want to use the place as a background, you'd better have a good close look at it.'

'I suppose that means you'll expect me to ride a horse.'

Blase grinned hardheartedly. 'No, I'll take the Rover; we can get most places in that and the few we can't we'll walk to.'

He and Merrin laughed at the horror which overspread Ellis's face.

'Have another cup of tea,' Merrin suggested soothingly. 'And don't try to fool Blase into thinking you're a ninety-pound weakling. I've no doubt he knows that you're the top of the squash ladder.'

'Now why should I know that?'

Hazel eyes met green, clashed and held. 'You seem to know most things,' Merrin pointed out softly.

Blase lifted his brows, derision sharpening his glance. Acutely aware of Ellis's shrewd intelligence taking everything in, Merrin cursed herself for being so quick to taunt. The last thing she wanted was to have him worried about her welfare.

It hurt, but she laughed, drawing with some shame on her physical attraction as she said lightly, 'Don't look so belligerent, Blase. It was a very mild jibe at your self-sufficiency. You should know by now that there's nothing more exasperating to women than to see a man who can manage happily without them.'

As a diversion it worked. Ellis grinned and made some comment and the topic swung away to other, less controversial subjects, but one glance at Blase had

shown her that he had not been fooled. He knew now
that he had a weapon in her concern for Ellis and his
narrow smile told her that it was one he would not hesi-
tate to use. At least he did not know of that humiliating
desire he had managed to evoke last night when for an
instant she had been tempted by the seduction of his
mouth and hands.

Even to think of it now made her cringe. What sort
of masochist was she, for heaven's sake! The interven-
ing years had not mellowed him at all; indeed, he was
an altogether tougher proposition now than he had
been then. Any woman who invited a second humiliation had to be out of her mind!

And if she needed anything else to protect her she
had only to recall Paul's face as he lay dying in the
hospital.

Pain racked her. She poured herself a cup of coffee
and sipped it, lowering her head so that her expression
was hidden.

'You're very quiet.'

She responded to Blase's comment with a smile.
'Mentally girding my loins for the day. Ellis, do you
want me to come with you?'

'You might as well,' he said generously. 'Give you a
chance to renew old acquaintances and I'll probably
want to dictate notes. You deserve a small holiday,
anyway. I know that driving me around reduces you to
a nervous wreck.'

'If you think my driving is bad you'd better take a
tranquilliser before you trust yourself to Blase,' she
retorted teasingly. 'If he's anything like he used to be
he'll take that Range Rover up vertical cliffs and along
river beds. With the rivers still in them.'

Ellis looked alarmed. 'I hadn't thought of that. You
always were a reckless devil, Blase. Is it too much to
hope that the years have given you a more healthy respect for your hide?'

'You'll just have to wait and see, won't you?' He
stepped back from the window, allowing his gaze to

rest a moment on the cool composure of Merrin's face before saying without any discernible change of tone, 'I doubt if I've ever been reckless, but whatever youthful follies I indulged in taught me several lessons. One was to think, hard and deep, before committing myself to any course of action. So you're quite safe, Ellis. I'll see that you and Merrin get back here without scratches or broken bones.'

Almost Merrin flinched. There had been no bitterness in his voice, nothing more than a hint of self-mockery, yet she knew that the remark had been aimed at her, a warning and a threat.

If the weeks spent here were going to be as fraught as the hours so far had been she would end up worn to a frazzle, she thought drily. Waiting for Blase to pounce was like being in a dark forest with a hungry tiger and only a sling-shot for protection. Watchful, nerves ragged, she saw beasts behind every tree, a hidden meaning in every remark he made, and always at the back of her mind lurked his threat to take full advantage of the situation. Why? To punish her yet again? Clever as he was he must know that she had no intention of letting him anywhere near her. And if he had banked on that physical attraction between them to carry the day her coolness last night should have disillusioned him.

But he had seemed almost complacent, letting her go with an ease which made her warily worried all over again. He had behaved as if all of the cards were in his hand, as if he had all of the time in the world to carry out his plans. Too self-confident by half, she decided, but the unease was still there, casting a cloud over the perfect day.

'Merrin?'

Startled, she looked up, met the ironic taunt of his glance. 'I'm sorry, I was miles away.'

'Can you be ready in half an hour?'

She nodded, but her answer died in her throat as he reached out and brushed her hair back behind her ear.

'I'll see you at the garage,' he said, tugged a lock gently and left them.

He moved quietly for so big a man, moved with the lithe purposefulness of the tiger she had fancifully compared him to, the wide shoulders set square above narrow hips and long legs. Today he wore his uniform of jeans and shirt, the denim revealing heavily-muscled thighs and legs. He always gave the impression of power, controlled now, kept leashed, but it was there, and with it was the violence she so feared, palpable and chilling.

'Magnificent physical presence,' Ellis remarked, pouring himself out yet another cup of tea. 'If he didn't have a brain in his head he'd still draw eyes. Even at school he had it. I used to envy him and think it was unfair for a kid to have everything—looks, sex appeal, brains and character.'

'Not to mention the money,' commented Merrin cynically.

Ellis shrugged. 'It's irrelevant, always has been. If he'd been born without a cent he'd have made it for himself. He's that sort. I can think of no one I'd rather have on my side in any sort of battle.' He grinned mischievously. 'Or who I'd rather have with me if we ended up lost in the trackless wastes.'

'What trackless wastes?'

He chuckled. 'Any tractless wastes. Unlike me Blase is superbly competent. He'd get you back if it was mortally possible to do it.'

'Lucky man,' Merrin returned lightly. 'He's got everything, as you say.'

But Ellis shook his head, frowning now, reflective. 'No, he hasn't. I had three years of marriage, the three happiest years of my life, and when Karen died I was able to lose myself in my writing. Blase——'

Jumping to her feet, she interrupted, disliking the turn the conversation had taken. 'Don't tell me he hasn't got feminine companionship, and as much of it as he wants, because I shan't believe you.' For some reason her hands were trembling; it helped to begin stacking the dishes.

'Of course he has, but he has no wife.' Ellis looked at her with shrewd concern, sighed as she whipped his cup and saucer away from him and said with a resigned note in his voice, 'I doubt if Blase believes there is such a thing as love, and so, while I may envy him his other attributes, I wouldn't change places with him.'

'I doubt if he misses any loving,' Merrin said drily. 'Now, if you're going to be ready in half an hour . . .'

'O.K., O.K., I'll go. You'd better arm yourself in case I want to take notes.'

Left to herself, Merrin stacked the dishes neatly, mainly to give herself something to do while her mind calmed down. Odd that Ellis's reference to Blase and marriage should have produced such violent response; for a moment she had felt as though she had been given a blow to the heart. It only proved, however, that she wasn't indifferent to him and she had known that all along. She had given herself away to Ellis, though. There was no doubt that he was interested in the situation. As a novelist he had to be. And kind and concerned though he was, here was a hint of professional ghoulishness about him which made her reluctant to reveal anything. He would not deliberately exploit her reactions, but she didn't like the idea of her most private emotions, however transmuted, being used as copy.

So she would have to make a greater effort, refuse completely to let anyone see beneath her social mask.

The decision made, she turned to go, and met Mrs Fieldgate, rigid, disapproving, her deep-set eyes curious as they scanned Merrin's countenance.

'Why—hello.' Try as she did, Merrin couldn't act with any enthusiasm towards this woman.

'Hello, Merrin.' The dark regard travelled beyond the girl to rest on the table. 'It's very kind of you to have stacked the dishes, but there was no need.'

Well, she hadn't expected a welcome of tambourines and wreaths and dancing; it was stupid to feel so chilled. 'My pleasure,' she said. 'I wondered whether you were still here. I was sorry to hear about your husband. Blase told me that he died.'

'Three years ago in January.' The older woman sighed, then said crisply, 'It was a shock, but he would have preferred to go quickly with a heart attack rather than linger. You look well.'

Compared with the depressing scrap of humanity who had run away from the station Dracula would look in prime condition, Merrin thought, her sense of humour suddenly flashing out.

'Thank you. It's odd to come back—I'd expected changes, but not the ones I've seen.'

Something showed for a moment in the older woman's expression, was swiftly suppressed. 'Well, changes are inevitable. I daresay there'll be more when Blase marries.'

Six years had done more than give Merrin a gloss of sophistication. They had given her self-control to summon at will so that she didn't move a muscle at this bombshell, beyond opening her eyes wide.

'Is he planning to marry, then?' Her voice was smooth and bland as cream with just the right amount of interest.

'We hope so.' Mrs Fieldgate began to pile the dishes on to a trolley. 'He's been seeing a lot of Coralie Allen. Do you remember the Allens from Patterson's Creek?'

'Yes, of course I do.' Merrin considered, head slightly on one side. 'Let me see, Coralie is the only child, isn't she? She was away at school when I left, but I'm sure I remember her. A pretty little blonde, with enormous dark eyes.'

'That's the one.' The housekeeper deposited the cutlery into a basket, and continued, 'She's a real beauty now, and a lovely girl. We're all hoping that they'll make the announcement on Blase's birthday. That will be in three weeks' time. How long are you planning to stay, Merrin?'

As if she didn't know! 'We might be here for his birthday, but don't bank on it.' Merrin smiled. 'It all depends on Mr Kimber.'

'Ah, yes. I read one of his books and enjoyed it.' A pause and then Moira asked, 'Have you been working for him for long?'

'Some years now.' Merrin's attention was caught by the chimes of a clock down the hall. 'Heavens, is that the time? I'd better go. It won't do to keep him waiting.'

'Him? Are you going out with Blase?'

A note of anger in the deep voice roused Merrin's resentment. It was no longer any business of Moira Fieldgate's who she went with or where. 'Why, yes,' she said calmly. 'Ellis and I both. I'll see you around, Mrs Fieldgate.'

Fortunately Hope always remained incommunicado in her room until nine o'clock so there was no chance of being delayed by her. Merrin dashed into her room, made her bed and returned the room to its former immaculate tidiness before pulling on a pair of fine corduroy slacks in her favourite claret colour with a long-sleeved twill shirt over the top. After a moment's thought she grabbed the matching corduroy waistcoat and a heavy cream pullover. It was a dream of a day, but clouds could gather swiftly even in such clear skies. It paid to be ready for anything.

However, it remained perfect, the kind of day to store in one's album of memories, green and gold and blue, clear and as hot as summer but with a slight breeze to temper the heat. The land lay smiling, serene and full of promise, the bush on the sheltering hills loud with cicada song and the sea glittered and sparkled as far as the dim purple islands on the horizon.

Slowly, as the day wore on, Merrin relaxed. Blase seemed to have forgotten the encounter of the night before. He reverted back to the man she had fallen in love with, in turn teasing and enormously interesting, the best companion in the world. His deep love of his land was evident, as was his extremely practical and scientific attitude towards the farming of it. He drove them over hills and down into valleys, leaving on occasion the excellent system of farm roads to get them to areas which Ellis wanted to investigate more closely.

Lunch was eaten on a low hill crowned with a grove of totara trees. The humming of bees and the occasional darting splendour of a dragonfly's flight provided an atmosphere of complete restfulness.

'Mmm,' said Merrin, licking her finger. 'Whoever made that pizza knows her stuff.'

'Moira.' Blase held out his mug for more tea, raising his voice to say, 'Don't tell me you're already exhausted, Ellis?'

'Not in the least. We creative people need more frequent rests, you know, so that our superb and ever-active brains can process all the information our senses feed into them.' And following this outrageous piece of nonsense, delivered in his most deadpan voice, Ellis stretched out on his back, an arm across his eyes, and proceeded to take a siesta, ignoring both Merrin's laughter and Blase's chuckle.

'I think I might follow suit,' Merrin said after a moment. 'My eyelids are telling me I'm tired.'

'Not enough sleep last night?'

She refused to look at him. 'Probably.'

When she woke it was to find a weight on her stomach. Dazed by the sun and sleep, she groped, felt hair and warm skin and realised that Blase was using her as a pillow. For a moment she lay completely relaxed, curving her hand into the smooth hair at the back of his head. An insect hummed intensely past, the swift drone forming a counterpoint for a cricket's slow mournful call. Sunlight dazzled in her lashes, golden-orange splinters so that she closed her eyes again and saw nothing but the red of her blood in the thin skin of her eyelids.

As if her movement had been a signal Blase moved.

It took the warmth of his mouth on her waist for her to realise that her shirt had worked free. Or perhaps he had pulled it away from her jeans to expose the smooth tanned skin there. His mouth was slow and sensual, warm against the warmth of her body, his head a heavy weight holding her to the ground.

She sighed, and he moved freeing her. One hand slid up to touch her breast, the fingers gentle as they found the hardening nipple. Darkness blotted out the sun; she opened her eyes, saying, 'Ellis——' and he said softly, viciously, 'No, it isn't Ellis, Merrin. It's Blase,' before his mouth covered hers.

For a moment she fought, limbs flailing, but he used his superior strength and weight to subdue her, pinning her to the ground with his legs and hands and shoulders, keeping her there while his mouth forced hers open in a kiss which seared through her body.

He hurt her, his fingers gripping into her flesh, his mouth crushing hers into nothingness. For long moments she stayed quiescent beneath him, the fear which he engendered locking her into a kind of paralysis. Then, as his head lifted, she remembered her vow never to be pushed around again and swift as a snake she lifted her head and bit him on the point of his chin, bringing her teeth together in a savage movement which almost drew blood and would certainly bruise.

He swore, his hands fastening on to her until she thought he was going to maim her.

Then he muttered softly, 'I'll make you pay for that a hundred times over, you little bitch.'

'Just try it.' Incredibly, her voice was steady. 'Sooner or later you'll get it into your thick head that I don't want you. *I—do—not—want—you*. The thought of going to bed with you makes me feel physically sick. I was a child when you seduced me, but I grew up fast, and I'm a woman now. You can't frighten me into making love, and I don't react too well to force or sweet-talking, either. You just might be able to rape me, but I wouldn't try it, because I'd see you in court so fast that you'd wonder what

the hell had struck you. So leave me alone, will you. Just
leave me alone!'

Exactly what he would have done then she never
knew, for Ellis's voice called, and in one swift lithe
movement Blase rolled over and stood up, hauling her
to her feet. By the time Ellis came up over the hill she
had tucked her shirt back into her jeans and was leaning against the Range Rover while Blase was stacking
the hamper into it.

Ellis said nothing, but his shrewd glance went from
one to the other, as though he sensed the tension between them. Hoping that he would learn as little from
her face as from Blase's, which was totally impassive,
Merrin forced herself to ask him what he had been
doing.

'Exploring,' he told her cheerfully, and went on,
'Take some notes, will you? I've come up with
something good.' Adding with characteristic caution,
'I think.'

As they drove down towards the beach Merrin found
herself wondering just what had provoked that onslaught. When she had woken she had forgotten the
facts of the present situation. For several moments she
had been transported back in time, and Blase's head
on her stomach had been as familiar as the feel of his
hair between her fingers.

No doubt he thought her willing. Shame enveloped
her as she remembered the wild sweet sensations which
his hands and mouth had caused within her. A time
shift; for those few minutes she had been the young
girl who had loved him so ardently that she allowed
him to do anything with her.

And then she had remembered Ellis, and had
muttered his name, intending to ask where he was. And
that was when he had turned savage. Not jealousy, she
thought dully, or if jealousy it was a kind of primitive,
unreasoning emotion which should have no part in the
make-up of such a sophisticated man. No, he was
intensely possessive, and because he had branded her

with his mark those years ago he loathed the idea of anyone else taking his place in her life.

For a moment she toyed with the idea of using his suspicion as protection, but she knew she could not. It was unfair to Ellis; somehow she would have to convince Blase that there was nothing between her employer and herself because if she didn't it could well be the end of their friendship. And such a futile end, she thought angrily. When she left Blackrocks he would forget her as easily as he had done before, his desire for her once more quiescent.

Especially if Moira Fieldgate was right and he intended to marry Coralie Allen. Merrin could remember her as a pert, slender girl already showing the promise of great beauty. The Allen family was an old one, well-connected and wealthy. Coralie would be a perfect mistress for Blackrocks.

A niggle of something hurt.

'Got a headache, Merrin?'

Even through a rear-view mirror he saw too much. 'No,' she replied calmly through lips reddened by his attack. 'No, I rarely get headaches.'

'Or any other sort of aches, thank goodness.' Ellis was almost hearty. 'The healthiest secretary I've ever had.'

Ellis was not a hearty type, his tone of voice must be prompted by the tension in the atmosphere. Oh, Merrin thought desperately, why ever did I come back?

The afternoon passed, still gloriously fine, but the grace had been taken from the day. Merrin found herself looking forward to their arrival at the homestead. At least she would be able to get away from Blase's immediate vicinity.

But then they pulled in at the homestead yard Blase asked blandly, 'Do you think you could drive this thing, Ellis?'

'If I absolutely had to.' Ellis's voice revealed his reservations. 'Why?'

'There may be occasions when you want to go out

and I won't be here to take you.'

'In that case Merrin can do the driving. I like to look around the countryside, not try to work out which gear I'm in.'

Blase grinned. 'I think I might forbid you the keys, anyway. Remember the time you borrowed your uncle's Jag and put it over a bridge?'

'Do I ever! I've never been able to look him in the face since. And he's certainly never wanted to set eyes on me again.'

'Right, then. If you'd like to change places with Merrin I'll put her through her paces.'

Ellis half turned, eyeing Merrin with some concern. 'I think I might get out at the homestead, if that's all right by you, my dear? I want to check some things out.'

It wasn't all right, but of course she smiled and nodded, and when they stopped at the homestead she slid in behind the wheel and under Blase's tuition took the big heavy thing through its paces. To someone who had grown up driving every piece of equipment on the station, including the bulldozer in the quarry, the Rover was easy.

After a few minutes Blase commanded curtly, 'Right, take it down the race to the lagoon gate and we'll see how you go in the rough stuff.'

The rough stuff was a nook of low sand-dunes laced together by tough scrubby growths which lay between a band of pine trees and the shore. It had been set up as a scramble course, Blase told her, for some of the teenage youths on Blackrocks and the surrounding properties to find out just what they and their motor-cycles were capable of.

'Take it through there,' he told her now, pointing out a track. 'Let's see how much you remember.'

It was hard to concentrate with him beside her watching her every movement, but she did, banishing him from her mind while she steered the Rover carefully around the obstacles. Surprisingly for such a big vehicle it was easy to manage, not too heavy on the wheel and its manoeuvrability and ability to climb steep faces gave her confidence even through the sand.

'Follow the track,' he said after he had directed her around the dunes for some minutes. 'It takes us through the pines and back up to the paddocks.'

Beneath the trees the air was cool and dry, slumbrous with cicadas and the occasional muted chirp of a sparrow. The tang of pine balsam was refreshing. Merrin negotiated the steep rutted track with a confidence which let her down when the rear wheels slewed on a sandy patch and she was too slow to correct the skid.

'Damn!' she muttered as the Rover stalled. 'Sorry about that.'

The broad shoulders moved in a shrug. 'You've done well,' he said indifferently. 'You always had a knack with machinery.' His hand stretched out to cover hers as she went to turn the engine back on. 'Leave it. I think it's time we had a talk, don't you?'

Merrin sighed, refusing to meet his eyes. 'There's nothing to talk about, Blase. Why won't you let the past die?'

'It was dead until you came back.'

She pulled her hand free of his and leaned forward, elbows on the steering wheel, her profile outlined against the sombre greenery of the trees.

'When I left here,' she said half under her breath, 'I thought that I could never be happy again. Well, never is a long day, and I've managed to get there again and I'm not going to jeopardise it by getting tangled up with you lot again.' An unconscious note of pleading made itself heard in the soft voice. 'Don't try to hurt me any more, Blase. You had your revenge—a harsher one than ever you'll know—for what you thought I did. You don't really want me. It's just that you think I should be put back in my place.'

'Which is?'

She bit her lip. 'Sexual slave. That was all that I was to you.'

He moved turning to face her and when he spoke his voice was lazy, almost goodhumoured. 'It didn't take you long to get over your unhappiness, did it? Within six weeks of leaving here you were married.'

Almost guiltily she moved to cover the thin gold wedding band which was all that Paul had been able to afford. As if the movement broke through his rigid self-control he hit her hand away, picking up the offending finger in a grip which made her wince.

'*Blase!*'

'What was he like?' he asked brutally. 'I put a private detective on to find you, but it took him three months and by then you were well married.'

'You—*what?*'

'You heard.' He began turning the wedding ring, pushing it around on her finger.

'But why?'

He looked at her, his eyes hard and angry. 'Because I hadn't finished with you.'

'Oh, for heaven's sake!' Furious at his arrogance, she tried to jerk free from his grip. His fingers tightened and the ring slid down. Moving so swiftly that she flinched back, he threw it out of the window into the undergrowth.

Merrin cried out, fumbling for the door handle.

'Leave it,' he snarled. Long fingers caught in her hair, holding her still.

Pain and shock brought tears to her eyes. 'Why did you do that?' she whispered. 'That was all that I have left of Paul.'

'Don't forget your memories.' His hands slid to her shoulders, pulled her across the seat to his side. When she struggled he hurt her, muttering, 'Stay still, you little devil!' in such a threatening voice that she gave up trying to get free.

'Good. Now, just sit quietly and we'll have that talk we need to clear the air. Tell me about your marriage.' His voice was remorseless, level and unfeeling.

Merrin shrank as far from him as she was able. 'What

do you want to know?' she asked wearily, keeping her head averted.

'Where did you meet him?'

'I worked in a restaurant. He used to come in.'

'And fancied you. Poor fool! Did he know that you'd already slept with two men when he asked you to marry him?'

Cold outrage stiffened her backbone, imbued her voice with an icy reserve. 'He knew that I wasn't a virgin. I hope you're getting a big kick out of this, Blase; I hadn't realised that one of your ways of getting thrills was to force confessions from women about their sex life.'

He laughed softly. 'Just you, Merrin, my darling. Did you sleep with him?'

'Oh, Blase! We were married! Of course I slept with him.'

'I hope he satisfied your wanton little body.' Very slowly he began to fondle the fine skin at the nape of her neck, the long fingers moving with an erotic sureness of touch which had her bitting her lips. He had forgotten nothing of the ways he had used to arouse her, the discoveries they had made about each other's desires in the nights they had spent together.

'Did you teach him to do this?' he asked softly. 'And this?'

His other hand slid beneath her shirt, finding her breast, sliding over the thin soft material of her bra to cup it, stroking and smoothing the sensitive mound until she felt desire like a hot surge of flame through her veins. For a moment she relaxed against him. A swift movement swept the dark hair away from the nape of her neck and he bit into the golden skin gently, his mouth moving along the line of her shoulder until she stirred, moaning, *'No . . .'*

'Yes,' he said deeply, turning her completely so that she could see the sensual satisfaction in his expression. 'You do want me, Merrin, admit it.'

She shook her head fiercely, her cheeks flushed with

the effort of damping down the fire he had lit deep within her. 'It's not just you,' she said, forcing the lie to sound like the truth. She knew that she was lost once he realised that he was the only man who could make her feel like this. 'You're not the only one.'

'I know that.' The insult was brutal, sped on its way with a smile which broadened as he saw it strike home. 'I'm not so conceited,' he said softly. 'Women like you are two a penny, my darling, driven by a hunger you can't control.'

'A hunger you aroused.' It was useless and possibly dangerous to deny his imputation even though the thought of it made her feel sick.

'Did I?' That cold smile derived her. 'Was I the first, or had Terry been there before me?'

Something snapped. A moment later she was as pale as he, noting with horror and fascination the marks of her hand on his cheek, white at first and then reddening swiftly. But she would not crumble before the hot rage which fired his green-gold eyes, straightening his mouth into a thin cruel line.

'You deserve that,' she said through lips which barely moved. 'I don't care what you think of me now, but you have no right to imply that I was promiscuous then. We made love because I loved you and could deny you nothing.' Slow tears forced themselves beneath her lids. Angrily she wiped her eyes with the back of her hand, ignoring him and the fierceness of his fingers on her shoulders. After a moment she resumed, 'You took everything else away from me, but you're not going to take that. I know that you didn't love me, but believe me, I loved you as much as it's possible for a kid of seventeen to love anyone.'

'Yet you married very soon after you ran away.'

'So I did.' Angered and humiliated, she drew in a deep breath, hiding the stormy green depths of her eyes with he lashes. 'Oh, for heaven's sake leave it,' she said tiredly. 'What use is all this? Endlessly re-hashing a sordid incident we'd both better forget isn't going to do either of us any good.' She looked up at him, saw the anger and contempt in his expression and looked away again quickly. 'Especially as I believe you're intending to marry in the near future. Coralie Allen, isn't it?'

'Who told you that?'

'Moira Fieldgate.' She laughed. 'I think she was warning me off. If only she knew! I know too much about you to even think of trusting my future to you.'

'Are you planning to trust it to Ellis?'

At her silence he lifted her chin, his glance piercing as a sword to the heart. 'Well, Merrin?'

'No,' she told him bluntly, remembering her decision of a few hours ago.

The probing, lancing gaze softened into cynical disbelief. 'And yet he tells me that you pander to his ill-temper in the mornings and wonders aloud why he doesn't marry you. It sounds as though you and he know each other very well.'

'We do.' She made to move away, but he held her without effort, his fingers lying loosely around her throat. If she struggled he would have no hesitation in hurting her again. 'But I am not his mistress, never have been and don't intend to be, and I'm not planning marriage to anyone.'

'Just as well. He wouldn't marry you anyway. His first marriage was idyllically happy. Fortunately she died before the gilt wore off. I think he'll probably want the same sort of all-encompassing emotion before he embarks on a second venture.'

'My but, you're a cynic!' Merrin breathed, appalled at the hard sarcasm in his tones.

Blase smiled and her blood ran cold. 'I had the best teacher in the world,' he told her, and bent his head and crushed her lips beneath his, almost suffocating her with his hot exploration of her mouth.

When at last he lifted his head, her mouth was swollen and red in a face white with fury and suppressed desire. 'Oh, I loathe you!' she spat.

He laughed with insolent scorn, his glance ranging the devastation his kiss had caused. 'But you want me, my darling. I know you too well not to read the signs. You can hold yourself rigid in my arms and refuse to respond to my kisses, but your skin is damp and your body moves involuntarily against mine.' His mouth straightened, became ruthless. 'Now, get this thing started and take us home. You can take it out any time provided you let me know where you're going.'

CHAPTER FOUR

THERE followed a time of peace. Ellis was well away with the book, keeping Merrin busy all day. In the evenings Blase was the perfect host, a little remote towards Merrin, much to her relief. He enjoyed planting little barbs of poison beneath her skin, but only she recognised them. Gradually the tensions built up by his attack relaxed. She would never be at ease with him, but she began to hope that the cool logical brain which co-existed with his strong passions had realised how unrewarding any resumption of their former relationship would be.

A dinner party was arranged. On that evening Merrin worked a little later than usual and had to hurry with her preparations. She decided to wear what she called her secretary's dress, a soft pink affair with a triangular yoke and long full sleeves above a gored skirt. It was elegant and inconspicuous. Her hair she pulled back from her face, and clipped at her nape, not realising that this emphasised neat classical features and perfect skin. On her feet she wore sandals which gave full value to slender ankles. Make-up of the discreetest kind and garnet earrings completed her toilette.

Staring at her reflection, she nodded, her eyes on the narrow white band where Paul's ring had rested. A long search early one morning had failed to discover it. Her lips twisted in pain. Impulsively she took her mother's wedding ring from her trinket box and slipped it on. Now it seemed as though her husband was really dead, all traces of him erased, and guilt darkened her eyes. It she had her life to live over again how differently she would act, she thought, and then with a steely determination, no more self-pity or guilt.

69

Not ever again. All she had to do in future was to make sure that she never behaved in such a way again, thoughtlessly, driven by pain and bitter anguish to hurt both herself and others. Had she not married Paul he would be alive today, probably married to a wife who truly loved him, with children of his own.

Instead he had died, taking his own life because he could no longer live with what his jealousy and her lack of love had driven him to become.

With the soft curve of her mouth set into a controlled line, Merrin left her beautiful soulless room and made her way along to the drawing room.

'You look very fierce,' Blase said quietly into her ear when she walked in.

It was the first remark of anything like a personal nature he had passed since the day she had tried out the Range Rover, and it made Merrin wary.

'Just thinking,' she returned without emphasis, looking around the room, her lashes discreetly veiling her eyes.

'Bad thoughts?' The lifted brow teased her.

She shrugged. 'Sad thoughts. But gone now.'

'Can you banish them—just like that?' His fingers snapped, attracting attention to them, she small, with a fragile air which was contradicted by the strength of character in her features, he big and fair and lithe, very much the dominant male.

'Not quite as quickly.' He was too close for comfort, but she refused to step back. After all, if he didn't mind giving the impression that they were indulging in a tête-à-tête, why should she care? 'But they go. Dwelling on the past can be a kind of self-pity.'

'And you don't indulge in self-pity.' It was a statement, not a question.

'I try not to.'

He took her arm, turned her to face the other occupants of the room who stood in a group before the French windows. 'Come and renew your acquaintance with the Allens.'

Before they were halfway across the room Merrin felt the intense hard glare from one pair of dark eyes. Coralie Allen had more than fulfilled her earlier promise of great beauty. Tall and slender, with an exquisite face and colouring, her looks were only marred by the mutinous expression she had assumed when she saw Blase touch Merrin.

Don't worry, Merrin felt like telling her, he's all yours, and I hope you're as hard as he is, because you'll need to be.

The Allen parents didn't look much older. For the moment they seemed undecided on the right attitude to adopt. The old patronising attention was no longer appropriate, but she could see that it pricked a little to accept her as one of themselves. In the end they were forced to, for Blase and Ellis made it quite clear that she was as much a guest there as anyone else. The younger Merrin would have been thrilled at such a recognition of her position; now she felt an amused sympathy for them set herself out to be charming.

Thank heavens for six years and a little sophistication, she thought an hour or so later. Coralie Allen could certainly do with some of both. The younger girl was behaving foolishly, her slender fingers almost always on Blase's arm, so totally absorbed in him that when he moved away her eyes followed, her hunger plain for all to see.

Merrin found herself feeling sorry for the girl, and extremely angry with Blase. He could stop Coralie from making such an exhibition of herself, but he seemed to be encouraging her. His green-gold glance rested frequently on the exquisite features, his smile teased her so that by the time the twelve of them sat down to dinner Coralie's cheeks were flushed and her eyes were bright and over-excited. Merrin saw Mrs Allen look at her daughter, then slant a satisfied glance at her husband, and hoped fervently that they knew exactly what sort of man they wanted to marry Coralie.

To her they behaved with only as much warmth as was compatible with courtesy. Perhaps they had heard rumours of her relationship with Blase, or possibly they were just snobs. The other guests were new to her and easy enough to talk to, although one husband had a roving eye which threatened to develop into roving hands. Merrin had eased herself gracefully from the corner into which he had backed her, mentally making a note to avoid him in future, and stayed within Ellis's orbit until dinner.

Over the pear and walnut salad she remained silent, listening to a humorous argument which had developed at Hope's end of the table, a smile curling the corners of her mouth.

It faded a little when she felt Coralie's eyes on her, fiercely intent across the low centrepiece of hibiscus flowers.

'You look as if you're glad to be back,' the younger girl said clearly, her voice sweet as honey.

'I am.'

The dark eyes moved to the wedding ring on Merrin's hand, then flicked up to her face. 'Renewing old friendships can be fun, can't it, though I'm sure occasionally one is disappointed.'

So she had heard something to make her suspicious; the knowledge was there in her expression, wary yet aggressive.

Merrin's sympathy was tinged with irritation but she answered mildly, 'Quite often, I should imagine. People change over the years and inevitably grow away from one another.'

'And has that happened here?'

Lord, but she was transparent! Merrin replied 'No, but you see, I'm the only one who has changed. Blackrocks is just the same as it used to be, but while I've been away I've grown up. So if there's going to be disappointment it will be those I left behind who feel it, not me. For me, very little has altered.'

Her words fell into one of these odd little pools of

silence which shy hostesses dread. Coralie sent her a puzzled look before turning her head to look towards the head of the table where Blase sat, lean fingers curled around his wine glass, his expression pleasant but impassive.

'Did you hear that?' Coralie asked, pitching her voice just a little too high. 'Mrs Sinclair says nothing has changed!' She turned back, lifting her eyebrows. 'When there are new houses all over the place—even the garden has been altered. Not to mention the pool, and Blase has a new yacht . . .'

'These are all details.' Merrin was angry with the girl for allowing her antagonism to become so obvious, but she was sorry for her too. In the grip of a strong infatuation it was easy enough to behave foolishly. Who should know better than she! So she continued quietly, 'The people who were here when I was before haven't changed a bit. The land and the sea don't change. A few details here and there, but the bones of the countryside seem almost eternal. Although the sea has moods which alter from day to day it never varies. The two sure things in this world,' she finished drily, 'are that the tide is going to come in and that one day we'll all die.'

Coralie stared. 'Ugh!—that sounded—funny,' she said, shivering as though Merrin's words had struck a responsive chord within her.

'Are you a fatalist, Merrin?'

Blase's question was delivered idly, as though he was not really interested, but she felt the keen hazel touch of his glance on her half averted profile.

'I suppose so.'

He waited, but she refused to expand on her answer. As if her words had been a hint Hope began to discuss the changes which the years had seen in the garden and conversation once more became general. Merrin took little part in it, preferring to keep in the background. To a great extent she succeeded, but was made uncomfortable by Coralie's frequent dagger-sharp glances in her direction. Whether or not she knew of what had once happened between Blase and Merrin the girl obviously scented a rival now. Merrin found herself wondering if Coralie was obsessively jealous or whether she was so insecure that she saw all unmarried women as objects of suspicion.

Later, when they were drinking coffee in the drawing room she was given the opportunity to find out.

'How long are you planning to stay here?' Coralie's voice was a little abrupt as she sat down beside Merrin, but she smiled and was obviously making some effort to maintain control over herself.

'I don't know,' Merrin told her frankly. 'It all depends on Ellis.'

'Oh, yes.' The younger girl's eyes rested disparagingly on Ellis, who stood gesticulating widely, in front of the heavy olive curtains, with her mother and Hope. 'He's a character, isn't he? Do you like working for him?'

'Very much.' Merrin's voice was composed and colourless, but a note of dryness must have come through, for there was a flash of anger in the dark eyes watching her so closely.

'Is it the work that you like so much, or the man?'

The question was impertinent, but the girl was trying so hard to make it seem a piece of sophisticated chit-chat that Merrin felt again that disconcerting sympathy. It led her to answer more gently than she had intended.

'I like them both very much. Ellis is the kindest man I know, and the work is fascinating.'

'Oh—*kind!*' Coralie's gaze moved to where Blase stood, her eyes revealing only too clearly what she thought of kindness as a virtue. Very little, obviously, when compared to the more virile male attributes he possessed. A spark of excitement gleamed in the dark depths of her eyes as she smiled before dragging her glance back to Merrin's shuttered features. With a little laugh she said, 'He does seem kind. Do you think it's important for a man to be kind? If you were looking at him as a husband, say?'

'Very.' Merrin's voice was now extremely dry. Carefully she put her empty cup and saucer on to an occasional table before continuing, 'I'm sure I read somewhere that in a survey of married women about what attributes they wanted in their husbands the highest on the list was consideration.'

'I can think of more interesting ones,' Coralie retorted, obviously bored. 'Still, you should know. You've been married, haven't you? My mother said you'd been divorced.'

'No.' It was a coincidence; it must be, for Coralie's voice had dropped so no one could have heard what she said, but Merrin looked up to find Blase watching her and as she continued, 'My—Paul died in a road accident,' he said something to Mrs Allen and came across the room to where they sat.

It was pathetic to see that flame of excitement illuminate Coralie's face. Patting the sofa beside her, she said vivaciously, 'Come and give us the masculine angle on this, Blase. Mrs Sinclair's just told me that she considers kindness to be the most important quality a man can have in marriage. From which I've deduced that either her husband was such a paragon that she's going to have a hard time replacing him or he was the exact opposite and she's not going to make the same mistake twice. What do you think?'

She was trying desperately hard to be worldly, like a child displaying itself in a new party frock. Merrin noted the affection in Blase's expression, an affection which faded into something else when he looked past the lovely, laughing face to hers.

'He was very young, wasn't he?' At Merrin's nod he went on, 'The young are rarely noted for their kindness.'

Coralie pouted, effectively regaining his attention. 'I think that's most ungenerous, Blase! Don't you think I'm kind?'

He grinned, touched her cheek with a lean finger as he retorted teasingly, 'You're a wilful, determined little cat with a set of cruel little claws, and kindness is the last quality I'd associate with you.'

From the febrile glitter in Coralie's eyes as she smiled up into his handsome face she considered this a compliment of the highest order. Again Merrin felt that sympathy, profound and tinged with more than a hint of fellow-feeling. Once she too had reacted like that to his lightest touch, eager for him, her body and heart on fire at his nearness. She had always had to hide her emotions, for Blase had not considered it wise for their relationship to become public. Obviously the same considerations didn't apply in this case. Coralie was so transparent, her mouth and eyes avid, her fingers tight on his sleeve, the proud young lines of her body expressing a yearning which was almost flagrant. Heaven help her if he didn't marry her, for she was at the mercy of a desire which had her completely in thrall.

'Well, you're certainly far from kind,' the younger girl protested now, laughing. 'As for calling me cruel—you're a demon, and you damned well know it!' Her glance shifted, fixed on to Merrin's face. 'You look shocked, Mrs Sinclair! Do you think I'm a fool for falling for someone as ruthless as Blase?'

Merrin's lashes lifted as a scornful little smile pulled at the corner of her mouth. Her eyes were dragged to meet his; contempt irradiated their green depths as she said quietly, 'Everyone is allowed to be a fool now and then, Coralie. The important thing is never to make the same mistake twice.'

Ignoring the younger girl's bewilderment, Blase enquired smoothly, 'Like you, Merrin?'

A tiny shrug lifted her shoulders. 'I've made plenty of mistakes, but so far I've never repeated one.'

A moment of silence before he asked, 'Never?' The mocking inflection he gave the single word hung in the air, a challenge.

'Never,' she repeated firmly, her glance steel hard.

He smiled then, and looked down into Coralie's lovely, petulant face. 'Do you think it's luck or good management?' he asked, irony very evident in the deep voice. 'I wonder if anybody else in the world can make such a confident assertion?'

Coralie could hardly be blamed for disliking the turn the conversation had taken as it had been completely over her head. However, his smile brought her good humour back in a flash.

'No,' she exclaimed, picking up her cue. 'I know I make the same mistakes over and over again. I'm sure everybody does. You must be a paragon, Mrs Sinclair, if you can truthfully say that you don't.'

Merrin found herself annoyed and saddened by Blase's complete ascendancy over the child, for child she seemed. Perhaps, she thought distastefully, he needed such uncritical submission to feed his ego. But her brain told her that a man of his self-assurance needed no ego boosting, that the truth of the matter was that Coralie was lovely enough to make any masculine pulse beat faster and that as she was an only child the Allen station could be considered hers.

Deciding that she was not going to stay to be baited any longer, she smiled, her expression lazily goodhumoured, and said, 'Ah well, we all cherish our little illusions. Perhaps that's one of mine. If you'll excuse me, I'll see why Ellis looks as though he's preparing to launch into flight.'

Blase rose as she did and for a moment they stood looking at each other. Merrin's breath stilled in her throat, for deep in his eyes there was such a concentration of cold hatred that she felt the blood leave her face.

'Running away?' he asked, and the shutters were down.

Her voice was husky. 'No,' she answered, walking away with her head held high and her back so straight it pulled at all her muscles. For a moment pain hit her again, squeezing her heart so that her steps faltered.

Ellis must have been watching; his long arm scooped her against his side, then released her as he said, 'Too much wine in the sauce, Merrin?'

She laughed, forcing herself to relax. 'I think it must have been. Delicious, though, wasn't it?'

'Superb.' He grinned. 'Do you think you might be able to coax the recipe from Blase's redoubtable housekeeper?'

'You'd probably have a better chance than I.' Ellis was a good cook who prepared all his own meals and could talk for hours on the right way to prepare a soup. In many ways ideal husband material, Merrin thought, wondering not for the first time why she felt nothing more than profound affection for him. Total lack of the spark that was physical attraction, of course.

Involuntarily her glance swung to where Blase stood, his handsome face alight with laughter as he looked down at Coralie. As if she had sent him a message he turned and for a long moment they stared at each other, her eyes bewildered, his fierce and acquisitive. Coralie said something, then tugged at his arm, following the direction of his stare to frown at Merrin.

It took such an effort of will to turn her head and break that contact that Merrin's breath caught painfully in her chest; deliberately she concentrated on re-gularising the movement of her lungs.

'Want to go home?'

Ellis's voice was low, for her ear alone. She swallowed. 'No, to hell with it!' Defiance sparkled in her eyes, bringing pride and strength to irradiate her features. Smiling, she said sweetly, 'Just make sure you guard my back. There are too many knives sharpened for me around here!'

One of his brows lifted, but his glance was sympathetic. 'So I'd gathered. Everyone seems terrified of you.

What did you do when you were here last—make a habit of juggling with Molotov cocktails?'

'You'd think so, wouldn't you,' she returned with wry humour, watching as Hope came towards them, her expression schooled into a calmness which only just hid her unease. It occurred to Merrin that Blase's aunt might consider her a threat to the marriage she obviously was very keen to promote. Which meant that she knew of that old affair, or suspected it.

It would be amusing to tell her bluntly that Merrin would rather walk overland to hell than let Blase within her defences again, but of course she couldn't. Hope would be shocked to her conventional little soul.

Mockery tilted Merrin's lips as she said smoothly, 'Ellis was just wondering whether he could coax the recipe for that sauce from Moira.'

'Oh.' Hope looked startled. 'Well, you can try, Ellis, but I'm sure Merrin has warned you that she's very close with her recipes.'

'He could always play on her sympathies—tell her that he has to cook his own meals and anything to vary them would be a lifesaver.'

Merrin's suggestion was intended as a joke, but Hope took it seriously, nodding. 'Yes, you could, Ellis. But do you cook your own meals? I would have thought that a housekeeper would be very necessary for you.' Her glance flickered to Merrin's face, making the implication that she thought Merrin combined the job of secretary with that of live-in mistress.

Ellis told her smoothly, 'I have a lady who comes in every day, but she has a family of four adolescent boys and a husband who does hard labour at the mill. Her idea of a meal is almost solid carbohydrate, so I prefer to cater for myself.'

'Merrin used to be quite a good little cook,' Hope said vaguely.

Ellis's eyes danced. 'Was she? Have you been hiding your talents,, Merrin? Why don't you whip up exotic little lunches for me?'

'Because you keep me too busy typing,' she retorted, her nerves relaxing under his undemanding protection.

Later, when almost everyone but the Allens had left, she mused on the security she always felt in Ellis's presence. It was probably because there was nothing but warm friendship between them that he represented safety to her. Safety and kindness, she thought wearily, watching as he talked softly with Mr and Mrs Allen. Some minutes before Coralie had dragged a not un-reluctant Blase off to show her something in the library and with their departure some of the tension had eased from Merrin's nerves.

Quietly she walked across to the doors which led out on to the terrace, opened them and slipped through. It was a soft night, cooler now as autumn advanced, but as yet with no hint of winter chill in the air. Above in the thick darkness Scorpio spread out across half the sky, menacing, tail curled as it threatened the pale ribbon of the Milky Way. In the west Jupiter and Saturn were in conjunction, the one a hard white disc, the other paler and smaller, overshadowed by its giant companion. Below in the pine plantation a morepork called. Another answered, the plaintive cry belying the nature of the fierce little owls. Some night-flying bird screeched as it passed overhead; probably a migrating bird fleeing winter for the warmer climes of the Northern Hemisphere. Mournfully waves broke on the spit, recalling Matthew Arnold's poem 'Dover Beach'

But now I only hear
Its melancholy, long, withdrawing roar,
Retreating, to the breath
Of the night-wind, down the vast edges drear
And naked shingles of the world.

A shiver of anguish feathered across her skin. She had read the poem often when she was young, thinking that its elegant disillusion ending with the final poignant statement that only love made life bearable was an ex-aggeration. She felt now that he had understated the case.

Life with love might be bearable, but where was one to find such an emotion? In her youthful innocence she had thought the passionate felicity she had enjoyed with Blase was love but there had been no trust in what he felt for her. And Paul had offered her love, swearing that it was enough to overcome the fact that she was carrying another man's child, that her liking would be all that he wanted until she learned to return his emotion.

Even now she could not think of him without remorse and self-condemnation. She should never have allowed herself to be talked into marrying him. In mitigation she could only tell herself that Blase's betrayal and cruelty and her discovery of her pregnancy must have rendered her temporarily insane.

She had come to her senses soon enough, but in spite of all her efforts she could not hide her withdrawal, her instinctive aversion to Paul's touch, and what had happened had had all of the inevitability of a Greek tragedy.

Lost in her memories, she must have heard the voices for some time before they impinged on her consciousness. When they did she took a swift step sideways, behind the shelter of a swathe of creeper, hoping that they would go away. If she showed herself now they would assume that she had been eavesdropping ever since they came within hearing, and Blase would look at her with the contempt which flayed her. A glance revealed that there was no way she could get back inside without revealing herself. They were standing close to each other at the bottom of the steps, only a few feet away. It was something of a minor miracle that her first impetuous withdrawal had not been noticed.

It was Coralie's voice, high-pitched and petulant, which had broken into her reverie.

'Get rid of her, Blase,' she demanded. 'I don't like her.'

Blase's deeper voice was more difficult to make out, but he spoke soothingly, his arm around the slender shoulders. Merrin closed her eyes.

'She's all out to make trouble. I saw the way she looked at you! I know all about her and you when she was here before. She still wants you, Blase!'

He must have lifted his head, for his next words were clear—too clear for one unwilling listener. 'You have no need to be jealous, Coralie.'

'I don't believe you. Oh, I know you couldn't care less, she's not all that good-looking, but I'm sure she's still in love with you.'

He laughed. 'What an imagination!'

'Don't patronise me!' Coralie's voice was shrill with anger and a kind of desperation which Merrin recognised.

She could listen no longer. With fingers pressed to her ears she lowered her head and clenched her eyes shut, willing them to go away.

Perhaps her thought waves did persuade them to move. After a few more minutes their voices died away. Cautiously Merrin opened her eyes, saw that she was alone and slipped back through the doors, her heart hammering in her breast as though she had been burgling the house.

Shortly afterwards they arrived back in the drawing room. A quick glance showed that Blase had managed to allay his companion's jealous fears, for she was flushed and radiant, holding on to his arm with the peculiar intimacy of a woman who has just been kissed witless.

Bully for him, Merrin thought crisply, barely hiding her contempt. Within a few minutes the Allens decided to go. Hope and Blase accompanied them to the door, leaving a room suddenly silent. Merrin sighed and turned to Ellis.

'There's something in the transcript you'd better check,' she began, and then stopped, as a small uproar began outside the front door.

'The *enfant terrible*,' Ellis murmured in his execrable French accent.

Merrin smiled, looking at him from beneath her lashes. 'She's very beautiful,' she said softly.

'She's too big for her brain.' He laughed at her shocked expression. 'Don't be hypocritical, my dear. You know damned well that inside that exquisite body there's a greedy, rather foolish child, and that's about all. Heaven help her if Blase marries her—she'll not know what's struck her.'

Merrin shrugged. 'I believe it's an accepted thing.'

'People been making sure you know?' He lifted his brows in a shrewd glance. 'I wonder why? They should know that with Blase nothing can be an accepted fact. He's his own master.'

'Well, if it's not he's an arrant flirt and he's going to break her heart.'

'Hasn't got one.' Ellis dismissed Coralie with a shrug. 'She's hungry for him, but his position and his money probably have a lot to do with it. I got the impression that Coralie sees herself as a lady of the manor, dispensing orders during the day and sating herself with sexual delights every night. Don't you think Blase deserves a little more than that?'

Merrin turned away so that his too perceptive gaze saw only the back of her head. A strange coldness in the pit of her stomach made her voice unsteady as she replied, 'Perhaps that's what he wants. Plus the Allen land, of course.'

'You really hate him, don't you?'

Light danced on her hair, blue-black as the sheen of a tui's wing. For the life of her she could not say the words, so she shook her head, hoping that he would leave this suddenly painful subject.

'Be careful, Merrin,' he warned soberly. 'Be very careful. Hatred and love are twin emotions, almost identical in effect.'

His arm around her shoulders was warm and comforting; she leant her head against him for a moment before stepping away.

To meet Blase's inimical glance, cold and scornful as he followed Hope through the door. Merrin's chin lifted. Beside her Ellis said lazily, 'What was the commotion? It sounded as though you were threatening to hurl her into the pool.'

Blase showed his teeth in a smile which came too close to being a snarl. 'She has a phobia about the dark.'

'Must be very limiting.' Ellis's voice was placid, inviting Blase to relax that air of watchful tautness.

After a moment he smiled, saying smoothly, 'Oh, not at all. She only becomes panic-stricken if she's left alone. Company eases her fears.' The hazel eyes moved to slide across Merrin's remote profile.

'Lucky girl,' Merrin said tonelessly. 'Not so very limiting after all.'

Hope moved into the breach, making an innocuous remark about the evening, then Blase offered a final drink which was refused all round, and five minutes later Merrin was with Ellis in the office clarifying an ambiguous paragraph.

Ten minutes after that she was back in her room, rubbing gently at the back of her neck. Yawning, suddenly as exhausted as though she had run a marathon, she took her clothes off, hung them up and pulled on a wrap. During the summer she slept naked, but it was almost cool enough to wear a nightgown; she hauled one from a drawer and stood for a moment pondering, but the bed was furnished with a down duvet which was beautifully warm. She put the gown on the bed. Shrugging slightly, she went into the bathroom and took her make-up off, peering at her reflection with eyes which remembered only too well Coralie Allen's beautiful features.

Not that her own were anything to complain about. She knew that she was attractive, even pretty, but beside Coralie's radiance she she faded into an anonymous background in spite of her clear olive skin and the startling contrast between her green eyes and the dark lashes and brows which framed them. Insignificant, she told her reflection severely, then brushed her teeth and came yawning back into the bedroom, one hand pushing the tumbled hair back from her face, the other clutching the wrap across her breast.

It was the yawn which made it possible for her to get almost to the bed before realising that it was already occupied.

Blase lay back against the pillows, hands linked behind his head, lashes lowered so that all that she could see of him was the handsome mask made by his features. He should have looked ridiculous among the satin and soft feminine colours, but he didn't. There was danger in every taut line of his body, and when he lifted his lashes and looked at her as, shocked and frightened, Merrin came to a precipitate halt, she felt a shiver of real fear.

Her chin came up. 'What the hell do you think you're doing here?'

'Waiting for you.' His glance was pure insolence, taking in her slender form from top to toe, discarding the presence of the far too revealing wrap to linger on her breasts and the long elegance of her legs. 'And you are well worth waiting for.'

'Oh, for heaven's sake, that line went out with Valentino!' She yanked the belt tighter around her waist as she stood, poised for flight, just out of reach. 'Will you please go?'

'Did you enjoy your spot of spying?'

At first she didn't know what he meant, but it took no more than a few seconds for her to flush in what must resemble guilt. Her eyes were unwavering as she said, 'No, I hated it. Not that I heard much. As soon as I realised I shut my eyes and poked my fingers in my ears. Believe me, I don't get my kicks that way.'

He didn't believe her, it needed only one lifted brow to tell her that, but his smile, derisive and tinged with contempt, underlined it.

Moving so swiftly that she had only time to take one step backwards, he came off the bed and grabbed the hands which clawed for his face, forcing them down and behind her back so that she was brought up against his body, hard and only too obviously aroused.

'You have a powerful effect on me,' he said beneath his breath.

Merrin jerked her head upwards, trying to catch the point of his chin with it. Blase was too quick for her and when, desperate, she tried to knee him in the groin he caught her while she was off balance and swung her on to the bed, holding her there by the simple feat of lowering himself on to her.

Her face was pressed into his shoulder. She began to think she would suffocate while his hands wrenched at her belt and pulled the wrap open. Panic-stricken, she bit into the hard smooth muscles, dragged her hands free and began to tear at him, gasping and sobbing in an agony of fear and hatred.

The big body shifted slightly, giving her air. 'Shut up,' he muttered, and lowered his head and kissed her.

He forced the soft skin of her inner lip against her teeth until she whimpered and surrendered, opening her mouth to his sensual invasion. Tears slid down her cheeks. He lifted his head and kissed her eyes closed, slipping his arm beneath her shoulders so that he rested on his elbow, only half on her, her body open to his eyes and his hand.

Merrin lay still as he traced the line of her jaw and throat with fingers strangely gentle after that first ferocious onslaught. The faint scent of the brandy he had drunk with his coffee was mixed with a subtle note of aftershave, emphasising the male scent she realised now she remembered as vividly as if it were only yesterday that she had lain like this in his arms.

Through lips which were swollen and reddened she said tiredly, 'Blase, please don't do this. You've hurt me enough.'

'You shouldn't have fought.'

She turned her head sideways into the pillow, chilled by the relentless note in his voice. 'Isn't that what rapists always say?'

'I'm not going to rape you,' he said silkily, his mouth stroking the line of her throat from beneath her ear to where a pulse beat a betraying tattoo.

Merrin's lashes flew upwards. For the first time she looked at him, read the implacable determination in his eyes. Fear kicked, cold and intense in the pit of her stomach.

'Then—what are you doing?' she asked, her voice thickening in spite of herself at the soft merciless touch of his hand on her skin.

'You'll find out.' He bent his head and captured her mouth again, but this time there was no callous wish to hurt, just a seducing sweetness as his lips explored hers. 'Poor darling,' he said softly as she winced. 'I'm sorry.' And his mouth moved slowly over her skin, gentling her, touching her as if she was the most beautiful creature he had ever known.

Desire, deep and strong, gripped her loins, ran like fire through her nervous system so that she gasped and fought back, determined not to be trapped ever again in its insidious spell.

'Don't——' she whimpered, her voice high and frightened as he moved his hands around her waist and pulled her higher on to the great heap of cushions. His hands held hers behind her back and none of her twisting and writhing could prevent his mouth from finding the sweet curves of her breasts.

He took his time about it, teasing, tormenting, girdling her narrow waist with his mouth, kissing the hollows of her shoulders, her throat and mouth, but returning each time to her breasts.

Eyes dilated, mouth trembling, Merrin stared down at the dark honey hair as his head moved against her. Slowly, so slowly that she was unaware of it happening, her small clenched fists relaxed. Blase made a soft contented sound in his throat and released his grip, both hands sliding up to support her shoulders beneath the wrap.

Merrin's heart thundered against his mouth. Shivering, taut with passion she was no longer able to control, she touched his head, her fingers shaking as they threaded through his hair, holding him against her.

'It's been so long,' he muttered, lifting his head to press kisses along the sweep of her throat. 'So long, my darling. Kiss me.'

This time she met his kiss openly, lost in the hazy mists of desire, her body responsive to every movement of his, wanting to lose herself in the ecstasy only he could rouse in her.

Her fingers fumbled with the buttons of his shirt, eased them free, and she ran her hands over the hard smooth muscles in an anguish of desire. Blase smiled against her throat and bit the lobe of her ear while she explored his body, driven almost mad by the touch of his hands on her stomach and thighs, tormenting, tantalising, erotically probing.

'What do you want?' His voice was husky; when she unfastened the buckle of his belt she felt him tremble against her.

Lost to all sense of self-preservation, she said, 'You.'

'Show me.'

Her hands slid across his back. She arched against him, pulling him down on to her. His arms crushed her; for a long moment they strained together in an approximation of the ultimate embrace, mouths joined, heart against heart, his loins hard against her hips.

Then he pulled himself away and asked harshly, 'Are you still certain that you never make the same mistake twice, Merrin?'

CHAPTER FIVE

ALMOST Merrin thought that her heart stopped beat-ing. She stared at him from beneath eyelids still heavy with desire before turning her head away, sickened by his arrogant triumph.

Her whole being throbbed in outrage yearning for his mastery, but hard cold pride came to her aid. Closing her eyes, she whispered, 'Did that flick you on a raw spot, Blase? Satisfied, now?'

His voice was very cool, but she heard the tell-tale thickness. However much self-control he exerted he still wanted her.

'No, I'm not,' he admitted, swinging himself on to the floor. 'I'd like to sate myself with you until I'm no longer roused by the sight and feel and scent of you. But incredible though it might seem to someone like you, I can do without it.'

Soft sounds revealed that he was dressing. Suddenly, harshly, he said, 'Cover yourself up, for pity's sake!'

'Why?' she asked softly, lifting her lashes so that she could see the stiffness in his hard face. He was looking at her, his glance restless, a hard flush of colour along the high, wide cheekbones. She sensed the hungry passion in him, the urgent need to ease his passion in the slender beauty of her body.

Cold anger possessed her. Slowly she pulled the wrap across. 'Having a struggle with yourself?' she taunted, swinging free from the bed before turning to where her nightgown lay in a crumpled heap on the floor. '*Poor* Blase. You really shouldn't start things if you're not prepared to finish them.' The mockery in her voice intensified as she shook out the gown. It was a cotton knit, an elongated body shirt, narrow and very clinging, dark blue in colour with red piping around

89

the high round neck and thigh-high slits at the side.
As if he wasn't there she slipped the wrap off and
pulled the nightgown over her head, smoothing it
down with careful deliberation, well aware that although she was covered from neck to toes every curve
and line of her body was revealed.

'Goodnight, Blase,' she said absently. She was rather
proud of herself for hiding so quickly the frustrated
disillusion that gripped her. Later there would be a
reckoning, but at the moment she felt triumphant, as
though she had wrested control of the situation from
him.

Gravely she linked her hands behind her back,
watching as he came around the end of the bed towards
her, big and lithe and extremely dangerous, his hands
tense as though he would like to strangle her. Hot fury
blazed from his eyes; there was a white line around his
mouth. Her taunts had destroyed his command of
himself. Almost she stepped back, but an instinct
stronger than fear kept her still, her head lifted proudly
while terror ran like quicksilver through her bones.

He looked as he had once before, when Terry had
told his lies, as though he could kill her. The blood
drummed in Merrin's ears as his hands fastened
around her throat. Without much emotion she thought
it would be like an old tragedy, to die at her love's
hands.

'Frightened, Merrin?'

She shook her head. 'No.'

He increased the pressure slightly. 'It's a wonder no
one has killed you yet. Your—husband tried it, didn't
he? What did you do to him, Merrin? Behave like the
tormenting, wanton little bitch that you are? Poor
swine. It's a pity we didn't meet before he drove into
that river. I could have told him you weren't worth
killing himself for.'

Her eyes dilated in horror. 'What—how did you
know?' she whispered, pale as one of the naiads he had
likened her to. 'Blase—how did you know?'

He smiled and her blood ran cold. 'I know,' he told her softly, releasing her as though the touch of her skin contaminated him. 'I know all about you, Merrin. Everything.'

He watched as she swallowed, desperately striving for calm. The remorse that overcame her whenever she thought of Paul made her sway. Numbly she sat down on the side of the bed, her bowed head exposing the vulnerable nape of her neck.

It was very quiet. The rest of the household must have been asleep for ages, for there was that peculiar deadness in the atmosphere which occurs when one is the only person awake. Merrin could feel Blase's eyes on her, feel the tension which sparked between them, and knew that he had won this round. But she refused to give up, struggling for equilibrium, forcing her rapid breathing into a slower pace, waiting until colour had come back to her skin before looking up.

Blase smiled again, slow, menacing. 'Does that worry you, Merrin?'

In tones totally devoid of emotion she returned, 'No. I've nothing to hide.'

'Literally,' he drawled, surveying her with an insulting slow scrutiny which brought flags of colour into her cheeks. 'You didn't answer that question of mine, my dear. Do you still claim that you never make the same mistake twice?'

She would have liked to stand up and order him from her room, for she felt too emotionally exhausted to cross swords with him. And too vulnerable, sitting on the low bed, with him looming above her.

'I can't think why you should be so determined to stress the fact that I find you physically attractive,' she told him, drawling the words with mocking lightness. 'You might have been the first for me, but you're certainly not the only one. And you want me, in spite of your smug hypocrisy.' She looked up, met the cold contempt of his gaze without flinching. 'After all,' she finished sweetly, 'I'll bet you've made love to quite a

few women in the last six years. Do you despise every
woman who wants you? Why treat me as if I soil your
fingers?'

'Is that a plea for more or a rhetorical question?'

Some demon of pain and anger forced a slow smile
to her lips. 'You'll never know,' she drawled, deliberately looking him up and down as though his only interest for her could be physical. 'I've no doubt that
you're an even better lover now than you were six years
ago. We could probably fan the embers and enjoy a
very satisfactory affair.' She lifted her lashes, smiling
at the icy disdain of his expression although her heart
quailed within her. 'But it would create a lot of complications,' she finished almost lightly.

'And complications you can do without.' His voice
was cool, hiding very effectively his emotions beneath
the tough concealment of his features. He too had
regained control of himself. They were still antag-
onists, still locked in a deadly struggle, but instead of
the brutal realism of a boxing ring the battle was being
fought with foils. Basic, primitive emotions were
hidden by a sophisticated mask while they fenced, each
seeking to disable the other.

'How right you are!'

Silence, the soft cry of a nightbird echoing eerily
above the softness of the waves on the spit. Merrin
turned her head so that Blase could no longer see into
her face, consciously holding her fingers still in her
lap. The lamplight glowed golden on the small neat
profile, emphasising the swollen ripeness of her mouth so
at variance with the control which normally marked it.

'Merrin.'

Her name dropped into the tension between them.

She looked up, saw something like pain sharpening
the hard handsome lines of his face. Her eyes slid away
from his. An unendurable anguish darkened them, but
she firmed her chin and lifted it. Too many years had
gone, too much had happened for them to be able to
reach any sort of friendship. Always at the back of her

mind would be the remembrance of his cruelty—and Paul's death, like a gateway barring the way back.

Sighing, her hands loosely clasped, she said half beneath her breath, 'What do you want? I'm very tired.'

'Look at me.'

It was a command, the cold crispness of it sparking off rebellion within her. With a flick of her hair she stood up, lifted her eyes and looked at him, searching for some small thing that would remind her of the lover who once had held her heart in his hands. Though her eyes probed there was nothing, the gay, recklessly vital youth had gone into the limbo of painful years.

'What do you want?' she asked again slowly, the words heavy. She no longer cared about hiding her emotions from him. Somehow it no longer mattered; they had gone too far for pretence now.

'You,' he said in a voice stripped of everything but stark hunger.

'But you're not going to have me.'

'No.' He smiled and the icy lack of humour frightened her. 'I wouldn't wish you on my worst enemy.'

'Well, we know where we are. You've proved your point, such as it was. Physically, I find you extremely attractive.' Her head lifted proudly. 'I hope you spend the rest of the night remembering just how much! Now, do you mind? I'm tired and I want to sleep.'

The imperious note in her voice made him flush darkly as though she had hit home in some sensitive spot.

'Don't speak to me like that!' he ground out.

'Oh—for *heaven's* sake!' Frustration sharpened her tones, made brilliant the green flames deep within her eyes. 'Just go away, Blase. You've had your fun, now leave me alone.'

Perhaps the defeated weariness showed through from beneath her momentary rebellion, satisfying his need for domination. His mouth lightened into a cruel sensual line as his hand brushed across her breasts, the fingers finding the sensitive tips in a caress without respect, merely cold desire and the will to humiliate.

Merrin whitened, closing her eyes in protest, holding herself erect in spite of an overpowering need to fall on the bed and sob her eyes out.

'No pert remarks?' Blase asked softly.

'No. Nothing.'

'So now we both know,' he said elliptically, and turned and walked from the room, undoing the buttons of his cuffs as though he thought of nothing more than getting himself ready for bed.

Merrin watched him, her eyes appreciating the lithe gait, the broad shoulders and the play of muscles beneath his shirt. Controlled power, yet, in spite of the fact that he was a big man, almost a giant, he moved with grace and smoothness. And as well, there was that aura of authority, the incisive, cutting mental brilliance which held his physical magnetism in check. *Control*, she thought viciously; he could bend even his desire to his will. He had fought his way back to sanity from a passion which had made him shudder against her in an agony of need. Oh yes, whatever else Blase Stanhope lacked, minor things like trust and compassion and tolerance, he made up for with that superb self-command. As the tears came she thought wearily, heaven help Coralie if ever she marries him!

For whatever else the evening had proved it was that he was not in love with the girl. Fond of her, no doubt, possibly physically attracted to her—what man wouldn't be, she was enchantingly beautiful! But however much self-discipline he showed he could not hide the fact that Merrin was still under his skin in the most fundamental way, a disease in his bloodstream. He could resist her, but he still hungered for her with a primitive, unreasoning desire that frightened her because she recognised its counterpart in herself.

Surprisingly enough sleep came quickly in spite of her overwrought condition; she even smiled as she slid into its welcoming darkness, for she had thought of

Ellis's hope that by coming back to Blackrocks she
could exorcise her ghosts. It seemed bitterly ironic
now. Her ghosts refused to die.

Of course nothing seemed so bad in the morning. It
was a soft autumn day, warm and clear, but the cliff
against the western sky was startlingly blue, so there
was the prospect of rain later on. Merrin rose early,
put on shorts and a top and her running shoes and set
off for a brisk jog down to the lagoon and back, hoping
that hard physical exercise would clear the muzziness
from her head.

It did, although her heart played tricks on her when
she ran past the pool. It was occupied. With a malicious
hope that Blase too had woken with a thick head and
aching with black frustration, she managed to get by
without him seeing her. As the pool was heated by an
array of solar panels on the roof of the cabana he swam
for most of the year. That and squash and riding kept
him in perfect physical condition.

She bit her lip, remembering that it was he who had
introduced her to squash. She still enjoyed the game,
was an ardent member of the club at home and kept
herself in shape for it by jogging around the enormous
playing field complex at the local High School. It was
years since she had ridden.

She had had her own horse, a mare called Korero,
small and black, with delicate flirtatious manners and
surprising stamina. Now she wondered what had
happened to her. Legally she had belonged to Blase, so
no doubt he had got rid of her; certainly she no longer
lived in the big horse paddock beyond the macrocarpa
trees. That had been one of the first places Merrin had
renewed acquaintance with, on her second day at
Blackrocks.

At breakfast she avoided addressing Blase directly.
It was not too difficult, for he had almost finished when
she arrived at the table.

One hurdle over, she thought, heading off to her
refuge, her little office. Ellis was well away on the book

now; she typed steadily, barely conscious of his pleasant voice in the dictaphone or the passage of time as
the words flowed beneath her fingers.

At one level her brain told her that this was his best
yet, taut, vigorous and crackling with excitement, the
landscape of Blackrocks coming alive as villains and
the hero fought an epic struggle over it.

So engrossed in her work was she that someone had
to reach over and turn off the tape recorder before she
realised that she was not alone.

'Why, Erana!' she exclaimed, as Blase's secretary
held out a mug of coffee. 'Don't tell me it's morning
tea time already!'

'Nobody could complain about any lack of devotion
to duty.' Erana's voice was dry. 'How's it going?'

'Oh, he's well away. Such goings on all over the
station!'

'I'll have to buy a copy when it comes out. Are you
going to drink it in here or shall we go out on to the
terrace?'

They had formed the habit of having morning and
afternoon tea by themselves, catching up on the years.
At first Erana had been reserved, careful not to touch
on anything controversial, but lately she had reverted
to her normal unrestrained self.

Now, sitting with the sun on her face, Merrin
wondered just how much was known of her relationship with Blase all those years ago. Last night she
had overheard Coralie say something that hinted that
she knew they had been lovers, and Erana's un-
characteristic restraint could have been due to the same
cause.

A flake of pink touched each cheek. Above the hum
of bees in a great swathe of rosemary bush she asked,
'What happened to my horse, Korero? I noticed that
she's no longer here.'

There was an odd tense little silence before Erana
said tonelessly, 'Oh, Blase gave her away, years ago.
There was nobody to ride her.'

'How many years ago?'

Another silence. Erana's dark eyes were fixed on a clump of orange tiger lilies, gay and stately, a vivid contrast to the clear blue of the rosemary flowers. 'About three months after you left, I suppose,' she murmured.

Something clicked inside Merrin's head. 'That would be about the time that he replaced the house where my parents and I used to live, I suppose,' she said quietly.

'Yes, around then.'

'And had the office and my bedroom redecorated.'

'Yes.'

And sold the boat, and had the swimming pool altered, because they had made love in the pool house and on the *Tokouru* and in her bedroom. The sun beat down on her face, but she felt cold, her skin clammy with shock. How he must have hated her, to systematically rid Blackrocks of every reminder of her presence. No wonder people had assumed that there was considerably more to their relationship than had appeared on the surface!

Conscious of Erana's swift sideways glances, Merrin forced a smile. 'What you might call a clean sweep,' she observed with a cool lack of emphasis.

'Well, yes.'

It was obvious that Erana was dying of curiosity, equally obvious that she was not going to voice it. Blase's actions had betrayed only that he wanted no reminders of her. No one could be certain why, just as no one knew why she had left.

Except for Moira Fieldgate, who was in Hope's confidence and who had made it quite clear that last week where her sympathies lay.

Erana sighed, lit a cigarette, and viewed the smoke from its tip with a jaundiced eye. 'We all got quite a surprise when you came back with Mr Kimber.'

'Me, too.'

'It was probably a good idea, though.' A faint flush

touched Erana's smooth brown cheeks, but she continued steadily, 'I mean, going back to your roots is a way of finding out who and what you are. If you can't decide what to do next.'

'I was quite happy doing exactly what I was doing,' Merrin told her wearily. She leant her head back against the high back of the lounger, closing her eyes so that the sun created orange and red patterns against her lids.

'Just being his secretary?'

'Just that.'

'Oh.' A pause, then her companion said, 'I thought—well, I'd hoped that you and Mr Kimber were thinking of getting married.'

Merrin's eyes flew open. '*What*?'

'Well, he's very protective of you. Moira told me that he watches you all the time. She hoped that it was true.' Erana's voice hesitated, before she said in a rush, 'I don't know anything and I'm not being nosey, but everyone knows you've had the rough end of the stick, your husband dying and everything. We all hoped that you and Mr Kimber would make a go of it.'

'No, I'm afraid not. Ellis and I are very good friends, but that's as far as it goes.' Merrin grinned. 'We lack that vital spark. I've never met a kinder, more gentle man, but although I love him I'm not at all in love with him.'

Erana drew on her cigarette, scowled morosely at it and stubbed it out. 'I'm trying to give them up,' she explained, not for the first time. 'Pity. About your Ellis, I mean. He seems a nice guy. Everyone likes him.'

'You can't love to order,' Merrin shrugged.

'Oh, ain't it the truth! If we could manage that I'd be in love with Blase and he with me.'

Merrin laughed, refusing to admit that Erana's joke came perilously close to being Merrin's desire. 'And leave poor Rui alone and bereft?'

'Oh no, I'd order him a nice rich little wife.' When

Erana laughed she flung her magnificent hair back and held nothing back, the rich sound enclosing Merrin in warmth and good humour.

'Kind of you,' she said gaily, and set her mug down beside her chair.

'Hadn't you two better get back to work?'

Blase's voice, clipped, with icy undertones, brought them both to their feet. It really felt as though he had thrown cold water over them. After one startled sideways glance Erana said cheerfully, 'O.K., Blase, there's something I wanted to ask you about this article you're doing. Can you give me a minute?'

'Of course.'

After that first coldly blazing glance he did not look at Merrin, but she felt his awareness of her as though it was a blow.

The little incident set the scene for the following days. Blase ignored her as much as he could, speaking to her only when courtesy forced him, and then always with an underlying chill in his manner. It was obvious that he despised her.

Merrin's own emotions were harder to understand. His lovemaking had forced to life again all the needs she had so successfully sublimated over the years; she found herself remembering the occasions when they had made love, recalling the freshness and beauty of their desire for each other, Blase's tenderness beneath the passion which she had aroused so easily in him.

Each day became a torment to her, packed with memories she could no longer subdue. Only when she worked, and thank heavens that was for long hours, was she free.

'You're not eating enough,' Ellis told her sternly over breakfast one morning. 'You can't live on coffee. Have you been for a run this morning?'

'Yes.' Aware that Moira Fieldgate was watching, Merrin took toast and spread it with marmalade. 'I went down the spit and through the pine plantation. It was lovely—clear and crisp, with fantails following me.'

'I like the way they flirt their tails as they fly,' Ellis said, eyeing the empty teapot with longing. 'You and Blase make a good pair—fitness fanatics the both of you. Only he swims and you run.'

'Would you like more tea?' Moira's voice was harsh.

Ellis sent her a startled look. 'Thank you, yes.' He waited until she left the room and continued in a lower voice, 'What's the matter with her?'

'Oh, she has moods.'

Ellis's bright glance slid over Merrin's downbent head. 'Ah,' he said, on a note of satisfaction. 'I coupled you and Blase. You must have created quite a stir when you left last time. I gather she doesn't want a repetition.'

'Moira has old-fashioned ideas on the class structure.'

'You could be right, but I'm tempted to think that she saw what your removal from the scene did to Blase.'

'You're a romantic, Merrin told him, cynicism hardening her voice. 'I've no doubt he gave everyone hell for a while; hurt pride is painful. But within a very short time he was having a wild affair with that Australian model, the redheaded one. Remember? She used to fly across the Tasman whenever she could and even gave an interview in which she just about said they'd marry.'

Pushing her plate away, she jumped to her feet, restlessness driving her to the window. 'And she was only the first one.'

'He's never married.'

'Coralie Allen. Sorry, Ellis, there's no romantically happy ending for us.'

Ellis sighed. 'Have you quarrelled with him?'

Banishing images from her mind, she smiled. 'If you could call it that, and you know damned well we have. So must everyone else.'

'I've never seen him so frigidly aloof.' Ellis smiled as the housekeeper came in with the fresh pot of tea. 'Bless you, Mrs Fieldgate. I need this.'

Moira's face softened as she looked at him. 'It's nice to see a man who enjoys his food and drink. Merrin, you haven't eaten that toast.'

'Not hungry.'

A frown creased the older woman's brow, but she said nothing more before she left. Merrin poured herself another cup of coffee and took it to the door, sipping it as she looked out over the lagoon to where the sea dazzled and beckoned. From a branch in the cassia tree a thrush sang, its sleek body contrasting with the vivid yellow flowers, looking like a mechanical bird as its beak opened and shut. A little black fantail cheeped as it darted to and fro among a cloud of midges, joined after a moment or so by another.

Slowly Merrin's set expression relaxed as she watched their antics; she smiled and felt that if only she could get away from this place she could once more remake the shattered pieces of her life. There was so much; the undemanding companionship of friends, the natural beauty around her, books, music, the well-being that her fitness gave her.

So much, and yet she would give it all away if Blase loved her as she had always loved him.

'Are you going to this party Blase was talking about?'

Ellie's question startled her. 'What party?'

'Oh, that couple who were here. You know, the McGregors.' As Merrin continued to look blank he elaborated, 'She's about forty, plump with a particularly penetrating gaze and an air of knowing much more than she lets on. She wore a blue brocade caftan thing. He's smaller than her, amusing and far from stupid.'

'Nodding, Merrin said, 'Yes, I remember them, but I hadn't heard anything about a party.'

'No, I remember now. Blase mentioned it last night

after you'd gone to bed. Apparently they've invited us
for next Saturday.'

'Oh.' Merrin frowned, touching a hand to her throat.
'I'd rather not go.'

'O.K. Well, we'd better get going, I suppose. Work
calls.'

The evening Blase broke his self-imposed silence by
saying, 'You're not coming this Saturday, Merrin?'

He had found her by the pool, watching the pink
and green fade from the evening sky as the night came
swiftly, blotting the colour from the landscape.

Merrin turned, her expression wary, her eyes sliding
away from too direct contact with his. 'No.'

'Why?'

He was wearing a dark shirt. Against the collar his
hair gleamed like honey, the sun-bleached highlights
emphasising the arrogant thrust of his head. Merrin
swallowed, torn by a wave of desire. Her skin warmed,
became heated so that she welcomed the soft dampness
of the dew heavy air against it.

'You, of all people, shouldn't need to ask me that.'
Her voice was husky in her throat.

'Because you can't bear to spend an evening in my
company?'

'What else?'

He shrugged, moving so that he stood too close to
her. 'So you hate me so much, Merrin?'

The lie trembled on her tongue, but she could not
give utterance to it. Very slowly, the words torn from
her, she answered, 'No. You know I don't.'

'That's the difference between us,' he said deliberately. 'Because I hate you, darling.'

She had never thought to hear him say the actual
words. For a moment an agony of emotion kept her
still; she could not draw breath, so locked was she in
pain. But pride lifted her head in the gathering darkness, pride and a fierce determination not to allow his
deliberate cruelty to cripple her emotions further.

'Tough for you,' she parried. 'Why? Because I was

the one that got away?'

'Perhaps.' His tone was indifferent, almost even, but so finely attuned was Merrin to his emotions that she could sense the dark menace behind the simple word.

Her attempt at flippancy faded. He had been hurt, six years ago, wounded in some vulnerable part of him so much that he could still only cope with it by hating the innocent cause. Her return had opened the scar, releasing the poison of years. Perhaps after he had humiliated her enough he would be able to love again.

Not Coralie Allen, her heart said, and she stiffened at the jealousy this aroused. Who was she fooling? And yet, if she could see him love again, his wounds healed, she would go out of his life happy with that. She had not intended to hurt him, but perhaps it had been inevitable. He had always been possessive, and where there is jealousy there is pain. What had begun as the ardent coming together of two people who thought that to want was to love could have had only one conclusion. It was Blase's self-esteem which had been shattered by what he believed to be her betrayal, and it had been further shattered when he discovered her marriage.

From down in the bush a kiwi called, high-pitched notes penetrating the damp air, primeval, forlorn. Merrin shivered, remembering. He had kept her a week after Terry's departure, reducing her to a mindless cypher, her only function to be humiliated in a sadistic parody of their love.

And then she had run, and compounded her sin by marrying Paul.

'I wish . . .' The words came without volition, without thought.

'What do you wish?'

The refrain of a song came into her head. 'More I cannot wish you than to wish you find your own true love this day . . .'

'I wish I'd never come back,' she said heavily. 'I was a fool.'

'You were, rather.' His voice was remote, cool as the

night air. She had turned away from him so that he could not see her expression; now his hand on her shoulder swung her back, too close for safety.

Eyes dilating, she looked up, unable to penetrate the expressionless mask of his features. Blase took her hand and held it against his chest. Beneath the splayed fingers his heart beat, heavily, speeding at her touch.

'See?' he said softly. 'Sexuality is a strange thing, isn't it? I despise you, and yet I'd give a few years of my life to take you out on the boat with me for several months. I want to indulge this degrading passion I feel for you, take you until I'm satiated, force your body and brain to give up every secret, to become nothing more than in instrument of pleasure to me.'

His voice thickened as his heartbeat began to race, from beneath heavy lashes his glittering gaze held her pinioned as it roved her face and body. The harsh muttered words sent desire like a hot tide through her, so that she trembled, her palms pressed against the soft fabric of his shirt. His hand over hers was hard, forcing her to recognise just how physically she affected him.

'Never anyone like you,' he said on a sigh, mouth twisted into cynical bitterness. 'Never since, never before. I look at you and like the poet said, I'm desolate and sick of an old passion.'

Oh, she knew how he felt, knew too the quotation. '*I have been faithful to thee, Cynara! in my fashion,*' she whispered, knowing now that for them there could be nothing ahead but the ashes of the dead past.

He smiled, cruel mouth without humour. 'Oh, that, too,' he agreed. 'Like committing adultery, each time a nasty taste in the mouth.'

'Yes,' Merrin sighed in bleak comprehension, remembering Paul and how she had hurt him.

He caught her other hand, brought them up to his mouth and kissed each one, his mouth hot as his tongue touched the soft palms. Merrin flinched, tried to jerk away and was hauled against him, his hands locking across her back so that she felt the hardness of his thighs against her and knew the heat of his desire.

'Don't,' she said on a high thin note of fear.

'I want to. Oh, *God,* I want to! And so do you.' His hand tangled in her curls, holding her head still. His mouth came down on hers as though by crushing her lips he could purge himself of the lust which was riding him.

Merrin twisted beneath him, flailing at his shoulders with futile fists until he caught them and pulled them down and enveloped her in that aura of sensuality which made her protests die.

Instantly the kiss changed, became no punishment but a seducing demand. Merrin's heart blocked her throat. She slid her arms around him and kissed him back, her body taut with need. Unknown to her she was making small sounds against his skin as he lifted his head to kiss the length of her throat; her hands moved restlessly over his back, pulling him against her until he picked her up and carried her into the darkness of the pool house.

Head back, eyes half closed, she watched the harsh profile as he laid her down on a lounger, not big enough for the two of them, but that was no matter, for he came down on her with a savage lunge, his legs parting hers so that she lay spreadeagled beneath him, his hands sliding beneath her shoulders to hold her still.

'What do you want?' His voice was thick.

Merrin's blood churned in her veins. Such impersonal lust frightened her. He was watching the rise and fall of her breasts as she breathed, his eyes gleaming beneath the long lashes. His hand moved from beneath her shoulders to follow the spiral of her ear, intimate, teasing.

'I want love,' she whispered, touching her dry lips with her tongue.

'Don't we all?' He lifted his head and smiled, staring at her with an enjoyment which drove the colour from her skin.

'Blase——' She hesitated, unconsciously wistful, and then the moment was gone. He pushed her shirt up and lowered his head. When his mouth touched the warm white skin of her breast a shaft of anguish impaled her. Her breath caught in her throat; she held his head against her and moved beneath him, remembering just how to incite him to the reckless passion which led for a short time to the perilous oblivion of ecstasy.

'Blase! Blase, are you there? Coralie is on the telephone.'

Hope's voice was high-pitched, agitated, very definitely coming closer. Blase lifted his head, his breathing harsh with frustration, his expression such that Merrin shrank back into the cushions.

Then he was gone.

CHAPTER SIX

MERRIN waited for half an hour, seated on the lounger, head bent as the darkness thickened and the dew fell outside. Crickets called, plaintive now that the nights were colder. Soon they would all be dead and the only sounds in the night would be the call of owls and the harsh screech of the pukekos, for even the noisy gulls quietened when the sun went down.

As the stars blinked and shone steadily she sat, thoughts racing around her head in an endless merry-go-round, until at last she pressed her hands to her hot eyes and wept silently, forced to accept that while she still loved Blase he felt only a devouring lust for her in which passion and the desire to punish were inextricably mixed.

'I must get away,' she told the unresponsive air, her voice heavy as she thought of what had so nearly happened only a few minutes ago. She had never considered herself a femme fatale, a temptress, but it seemed that to Blase she was just that. An insolent, primitive part of her warmed at the thought. He was so sure of himself, so much in command of his emotions and his life that it satisfied some anarchic instincts to topple him from his pinnacle of self-esteem.

Then she remembered the blind hunger with which he had caressed and held her, and shuddered. There had been no emotion in him, only a barbaric drive to satisfy the inborn need to perpetuate himself. He had been as driven by instinct as any male animal confronted with a receptive female.

So had she, caught in the thrall of the masculine sensuality he exuded. Had Hope not interrupted they would have been intertwined on the lounger even now, exhausted in the aftermath of passion.

Merrin bit her lip and clenched her fists, forcing back the images her thoughts aroused. She could not allow this to happen again. The night Blase had come to her bedroom had been humiliating enough, but this latest incident would have been disastrous for her self-respect, as shattering as his original rejection had been.

Six years ago she had become his mistress gladly, convinced that he loved her. Even his rejection of her story after Terry's betrayal had been understandable, for Terry lied with complete conviction and Hope had hammered home the final nail in her coffin. Young as she was Merrin had understood Blase's fierce possessiveness, his deep need to be the only one in her life. The real betrayal had been his refusal to accept her word before his family's. He had believed them, and gone on believing them, putting Merrin in second place, unconsciously revealing that although he had taken her he considered her inferior to the Stanhopes.

It was her rejection of his attitude which had driven her away from Blackrocks. In love there is no inferior or superior and she possessed a still, cold pride which refused to submit either to his sexual humiliation of her or his view of her position in his life.

So she had gone, and ultimately Paul had died, as had the little girl she and Blase had made together, and she and Blase had been left emotionally crippled. He had admitted that for him there had since been nothing like that first loving. She bit her lip again, wondering jealously what other women he had possessed besides the lovely Australian model who had thought to marry him. The thought of him wanting anyone but her was torment; it drove her to her feet and past the pool to stand in the shade of a jacaranda tree and watch while the moon climbed from the sea like a great brass ball to lose itself in a thick bank of cloud just above the horizon.

A faint wind sprang up, bringing with it the soft sound of a cow calling. Somewhere on the road from Blackrocks hill a truck laboured, the sound of its engine fading as it passed Appleton's station and went behind some low hills before reaching the coast well to the south.

Merrin shivered and turned back to the house, watching with jealous eyes as the windows flowered with light. Her throat ached. She loved it so, had always loved it, judged every home, every landscape, by this home, this landscape, judged every man according to Blase's standards and found them all wanting. Why had Ellis insisted she return? Why had she been so stupidly, idiotically, confident of her own strength as to agree?

Wincing with a chill which seemed to originate in her bones, she made her way through the sweetly smelling garden back to the house. It would be time for dinner soon and she had to shower and change. She wished she could develop a headache and look wan enough to make a very early evening reasonable, but a glance at her mirror showed a perfectly normal countenance if one discounted the bruised lips and heavy slumbrous eyes.

After a first glance sharp as a rapier Blase continued to ignore her as much as his courtesy would permit, but she was uneasily aware of Hope's pale gaze on her, and once, when the two men were at the other end of the room, she surprised a weary, troubled frown on the older woman's brow that made her wince.

Ellis brought up the subject of the McGregors' party and somehow Merrin found herself agreeing to go. She knew that Blase would prefer her to stay away, but there seemed no correct way of going about it. Ellis rather liked to have her there to rescue him from bores and act as his partner.

After dinner Blase said abruptly, 'I'm going out to shoot opossums. Care to come, Ellis?'

Ellis got to his feet with alacrity. 'Yes, it's years since

I've hunted big game. Can we take Merrin, or is this a strictly masculine pursuit?'

'Merrin used to be a better shot than most men I know,' Blase said drily. 'Merrin?'

She shook her head. 'No, thank you. I'm tired—I'll get an early night.' She hesitated, then asked, 'Are they bad up here?'

'Oh, we keep them under control. The bounty hunters use cyanide in the bush and shoot over farmland; several of the local kids help to keep them down over Blackrocks.' He looked at his watch. 'Moira will have left, I suppose. Hope, do you think you could get us a flask of coffee?'

'I'll do it,' Merrin offered, as Hope was busy knitting a particularly fierce Aran pattern jersey for one of her godchildren.

'Fine.'

The kitchen was as exquisitely neat as Moira Fieldgate herself. Frowning slightly, Merrin reached for a vacuum flask after she had switched the percolator on. While the coffee bubbled quietly she stood staring into the gleaming stainless steel sink.

Had Terry not needed money so much that he was prepared to steal it she might have been mistress of all of this—the gracious house, the wide, fertile acres, the man who owned them all. A small, hard smile pulled up the corners of her mouth. Mistress was probably the correct word. Blase had told her often enough that he loved her, but nothing had ever been said about marriage. Why should he? she thought cynically; he had all of the comforts of matrimony with none of the disadvantages. A willing, passionate partner in love-making, young and unsophisticated enough to play the game by his rules, too proud to stay around when he had made it clear there was no future for them.

What would have happened if Terry had not been there that night? What would Blase have done if she had told him about the baby? Perhaps he would have married her; she no longer knew. The Blase she had loved had turned out to be a figment of her imagination, a fairytale prince of no substance.

There had been an unpleasant awakening for this Sleeping Beauty, she thought ironically. And certainly no living happily ever after. It had taken this return to Blackrocks to reveal how she had withdrawn from life, too afraid of hurting and being hurt to trust herself in any but the most superficial of relationships. She and Blase had killed something vital in each other, the ability to trust.

Too late. The saddest words in the language. And self-pity, she told herself with fierce determination, was the most despicable emotion. She poured milk into a plastic container, sugar into another, and went out into the small ante-room which held odds and ends, took down a flax kit and came back with it. Blase was waiting for her, dangerous in a heavy dark jersey and trousers, the light gleaming on the smooth thick hair.

'Coffee should be ready,' Merrin said without expression.

He nodded, watching as she tipped it into the vacuum flask. The cold scrutiny made her nervous. Her hand jerked, and the scalding liquid splashed across her fingers.

Blase's hand shot out. Before she had time to think he had grabbed her wrist, thrust it over the sink and turned the cold tap on to the afflicted part.

Tears squeezed themselves beneath her lower lashes. She stood, head bent, as the water played over her fingers, easing the pain. Blase's grip on her wrist was fierce as though he expected her to pull away.

Then he turned the tap off and said brusquely, 'You'd better put a bandage on to protect the skin. It shouldn't blister, but it will be tender for a few days.'

'Yes,' she said, and then, incredibly, 'Blase, what happened to Terry?'

'Terry?' His eyes hardened then became enigmatic. 'He's dead,' he told her. 'He got mixed up in something unsavoury in Thailand four years ago and was found shot in a Bangkok street.'

'Drugs?' She could barely whisper the word.

His shoulders lifted. 'Possibly.'

'Oh, poor Mrs Grier!'

The deliberate lack of expression in his face didn't alter. 'Yes, poor Hope.' He had been holding her wet hand in his. Now he looked down at it and touched, very gently, the reddened patches. 'He suffered from a fatal flaw,' he said drily. 'He was weak. He had everything else, looks, sex appeal and brains, but they got him nowhere. There's no cure for weakness.'

It was a cool, dispassionate epitaph on a man he had grown up with. Chilled, Merrin pulled her hand free. For a moment she had been tempted to make one final effort to convince him of Terry's perfidy, but it was useless appealing to a man who could be so callous about his cousin's wasted life and tragic death.

'You hated him, didn't you?'

He lifted his gaze to her face, something inhuman in the depths of it. 'Yes, I hated him,' he agreed, 'and it was only for Hope's sake that I was sorry at his death.' A twisted smile emphasised the harsh lines of his face. 'He took the one thing I valued,' he said implacably. 'He lost me my illusions. I'd thought that love and faith and happiness could be found in one person, but Terry showed me how wrong I was.'

Merrin shivered, for his eyes hated her, despised her. 'It's a pity I didn't die too,' she said bitterly. 'I almost——' She stopped precipitately, biting her lip, then hurried on, 'Then you'd be free of both of us.'

'Yes.'

She turned away, furious with herself for making a slip like that. She had almost died when she miscarried their baby, had been tempted to let go and sink into the oblivion she craved, but some instinct at her most primitive level had fought for her, forcing her back into the world.

As she poured the rest of the coffee into the flask she felt his eyes on the slender curves of her body and beneath the pain and the despair she felt a reluctant response.

'There,' she said huskily, putting the flask into the kit beside the milk and sugar. 'Good hunting.'

'Do you mean that?'

An odd note in this voice attracted her attention. When she looked up she saw him smile. She turned, but not swiftly enough. His hands fastened on to her shoulders as he pulled her back against him. He bent his head, found the sensitive place where her neck and shoulder met and bit her very gently there.

A shiver of anticipation ran through her nerves. Aloud she said, 'Stop it—please, Blase.'

'Why? I like it—you like it. What harm is there?'

He spoke against the smooth gold of her skin, his lips erotically tantalising. One hand slipped beneath her arm and closed over her breast.

'No!' She twisted, angered by his contemptuous assumption that he could fondle her whenever he chose. 'What would Coralie Allen think if she saw you now?'

The skin over the high cheekbones tightened, the cruel mouth thinning into a line. 'That's none of your business.'

'It might not be, but it's yours. Let me go.'

Green eyes met his defiantly, refusing to surrender even though a betraying pulse beat heavily in her throat. His glance rested on it for a significant moment before he made an exclamation of self-contempt and released her, snatching up the kit as if her touch poisoned him and moving with rather less than his usual grace to the door.

Wearily Merrin returned to the room where Hope knitted.

'You look tired,' the older woman remarked, frowning slightly

Merrin sighed. 'I am. I think I'll make it an early night tonight.'

'Sensible of you.' Hope put down her knitting, the

pale eyes hardening as they came to rest on the demure lines of Merrin's face. 'Did Blase persuade you to go to the McGregors' party?'

Merrin looked up, startled. 'No. Ellis likes—it was Ellis.'

'Ah.' Her companion resumed knitting. 'You knew that Coralie is going too?'

'Yes.'

'Forgive me for asking, but are you and Ellis thinking of marriage?' Flakes of pink touched Hope's cheeks. 'I notice that he's very protecive of you, and you get on so well together . . .'

Unbidden, a small cynical smile touched Merrin's lips. Hope might just as well have come out and said that she didn't want Merrin upsetting her carefully laid plans for Blase and Coralie. Just how much *did* she know of what had happened in this house six years ago?

'No,' she said bluntly. 'We do get on very well together, but I don't think that Ellis has ever found a woman he could put in his wife's place.'

'A pity. And you—do you still grieve for the loss of your husband?'

Tears gathered behind Merrin's lids. 'Oh yes,' she said, very softly, 'I still grieve for Paul.'

'Forgive me—I didn't——' Incredibly Hope was at a loss for words. She coughed, then resumed, 'You must think me a crassly insensitive woman, but I do so want to prevent any—any more heartache.' Colour deepened in her cheeks as she carefully avoided looking anywhere but at her knitting. 'We expect Blase and Coralie to announce their engagement very soon. She's devoted to him, as I'm sure you've noticed, and Blase needs—he needs to become settled.'

Merrin felt sorry for her, knowing how distasteful this must be for her. The fact that she was forcing herself to explain like this revealed how worried she must be about Merrin's disruptive influence. Who did she think she had as a guest? Mata Hari?

Aloud she said quietly, 'I'm sure he does.'

But Hope hadn't finished. In a manner so at variance with her usual serene hauteur that she seemed a different woman she continued, 'Blase needs a wife who won't take up too much of his time. He has so much to do, so many things to control—well, you know from the time you worked for him. There's even more, now. He's an extremely busy man and if he had a demanding wife it would drain too much from him. He needs his energies for the business.'

'You don't think Coralie would be demanding?'

Hope shook her head. 'Oh, beneath that rather childish surface Coralie is a very sensible girl. She knows the life.' She stilled the needles suddenly, firming her mouth. 'Some women demand everything from a man; they want too much—his heart, his time, every waking thought and sleeping dream. Coralie won't be like that. Blase needs rest, not a wildly feverish emotion eating at him, giving him no peace.'

Merrin looked at her in astonishment. Hope spoke almost in anguish, all complacency gone. For the first time Merrin realised that Hope loved her nephew with the obsessive love of a mother. Whatever she had done she had done not out of malice but because she loved. Her instinct was to protect.

And who was to say that she was wrong? The emotions Merrin had conjured in Blase were certainly far from conducive to peace or happiness.

'Blase will be content with Coralie.' Hope was running on now seemingly out of control, the words coming swiftly to her lips, strangely unlike her usual measured way of speaking. 'And you—you must have loved your husband, to be still grieving for him.'

It wasn't a question. Merrin drew a jerky breath, understanding that Hope was as close to an apology as she would ever be for the lie she had told six years ago. She must have known something of the relationship between Blase and the daughter of the shepherd whom they had taken into the homestead. Her knowledge had been enough to see that by backing up Terry's story she could rid Blackrocks of the intruder as well as protect her son from his cousin's fury. But because she was not wicked, only thoughtless, she had been uneasy about the effect on Merrin. No doubt it eased her conscience to think that Merrin's emotions had been shallow enough to be easily transferred, so she thought, to another man.

A travesty of a smile pulled at Merrin's lips.

'What's the matter?' Hope demanded shrilly.

Merrin got to her feet, moving with unconscious grace to look outside. 'Nothing,' she said, regaining control. 'Nothing at all. I can see the searchlight out on the flats and I wonder if they're having any luck. I've heard two shots so far.'

From behind she saw the light flash on the needles as Hope began to knit once more.

'Blase is an excellent shot,' she said, her voice returning to its usual placidity.

'Yes. I think I'll go off to bed now.' Merrin unclenched her hand from the silk curtain, turned herself to meet that bland gaze. 'Goodnight, Mrs Grier.'

It rained the next day, cleared the day after that and the third day, unable to make up its mind, alternated showers with brilliantly sunny periods. Merrin typed crossly, wishing that she could get out into the fresh air and ease her fretted nerves with some violent exercise like leaping from hilltop to hilltop or swimming to Australia. Unfortunately that reminded her of her father, who had set out in his small runabout and never returned. She wondered if he had really intended to die out there. Still grieving from the shock of his wife's sudden death, he could have made the decision to join her. He had been a silent man, reserved, almost humourless, and his love for his wife did not seem to extend to their child.

A week after his last fishing trip his body had been washed up along the coast. Blase had identified him, comforting the distraught Merrin like a brother, and had stayed like that for a year, waiting until she was seventeen before he had stamped her with his seal of possession.

For a moment the flying fingers on the typewriter faltered. Merrin swore an unladylike oath as she corrected the mistake, then bent all her concentration on to the job in hand. She would not allow herself to be distracted; she owed Ellis only her best.

But although she managed to keep Blase from her brain while she was working she found it impossible at any other time. The nights turned into endurance sessions when she lay in her beautiful room, watching as the moon dwindled slowly from the full, unable to sleep, unable to banish memories which hurt as much as they excited her.

When at last she slept it was to be disturbed by dreams, fragments of past happiness, presentiments of future pain, haunted by a Blase who wanted only to kill her.

'You look how I feel,' Ellis muttered on the morning of the McGregor's party. He shook his head to flip back the lock of hair over his brow and winced, momentarily closing his eyes.

Merrin peered across the table. 'Have you a headache?'

'Yes.' He looked resigned and slightly guilty. 'I think I'm getting a migraine.'

'Have you taken your pills?'

'Uh-huh, but I suspect this is going to be one of the occasions when they're not going to work.'

Merrin's expression softened into sympathy. 'Poor old thing. Hadn't you better get back to bed?'

'I suppose so.' He stood, paling as the pain hit him. 'Can I trust you to guard the door?'

'Yes, of course.'

Ellis rarely suffered with migraine, but when he did he needed complete quiet in a darkened room for the twenty-four hours or so that they lasted. At least the tablets seemed to suppress the nausea. Ellis might have convinced himself that they didn't work, but Merrin was sure that they also took the edge off the pain.

'Come on,' she said now, getting to her feet and holding out her hand to him. 'Bed for you.'

It wasn't until she was pouring herself another cup of coffee back at the breakfast table that she realised the implications of Ellis's affliction. She would be able to stay away from the party. Now that Ellis was sick there was no reason for her to go. A sigh of relief ruffled the smooth surface of the coffee as she sipped it. Thank heavens she would be spared the sight of Coralie with Blase, those possessive little hands on his arm, the glint of sexual attraction in the younger girl's eyes as she pouted and smiled and chattered at him. For that she could be thankful.

There was enough work to keep her busy during the morning, but by lunchtime she had finished everything. Lunch was a quiet meal, for Blase was out on the station somewhere. Merrin responded to Hope's conversational gambits, before offering help with the dishes which was politely turned down by Moira Fieldgate.

An intolerable restlessness ached in her limbs. She changed into heavy corduroys and a thick jersey, pulled on a suede jacket and slipped out of the house, determined to walk it off. Hands scrunched into the pockets of her jacket, she leaned into the cold, brisk wind as she walked down past the lagoon, through the tangled growth of the sandpit and along the fine wet sand of the beach, watching the breakers as they gathered strength to fall on the sand. A south-easterly wind had been blowing for the last few days, so the waves on this unprotected coast were higher than normal and dirty with sediment. They pounded in, long lines of them across the bay, gushing up between the rocks at the foot of the headland in a welter of spray and foam, rising and falling in a rhythm as old as time, as soothing as a mother's heartbeat.

The wind tore at Merrin's hair, whipping colour back

into her cheeks. She shrugged deeper into her coat, turning the collar up to protect the nape of her neck, and walked on stubbornly, noting with a weatherwise eye a dark bank of cloud massing low on the horizon. The weather was due for a change; by the look of that it would not be one for the better. However, it was moving slowly, so probably the change would come during the night.

As if infected by the wind seagulls screamed and shrieked as they were tossed overhead, most of them heading inland in flocks—another indication of worsening weather. Merrin sighed, licked the salt spray from her lips and pushed on, impelled by needs she had hoped had died for ever to exhaust herself in physical exercise.

It was too dangerous to go climbing around the rocks at the base of the cliff. There was an incoming tide and the sea was high, so, reluctantly, she turned her back to the wind and made her way up the beach to where an enormous pohutukawa tree sprawled out across the sand rocks, its long tough roots binding together a high bank. It was easy enough to climb, but by the time she reached the top she was pink with exertion, using muscles that even her running didn't exercise.

At the top she leant against the thick trunk, breathing deeply. Out to sea a long tanker made its way slowly down the coast to the refinery at Marsden Point, evidence of man's technology in a wild waste of waters. No yachts on the sea today, no sign of any smaller vessels at all; they would all be snug in port.

Borne on the wind she could hear the high-pitched whistle of a shepherd. She turned, watching with pleasure as he worked a flock of sheep across the flats and into a paddock on a hillside. Obviously Blase was taking no chances with the weather; she noticed a mob of Herefords being moved too, out of the range of any floods. He too was expecting something from that cloud.

A further glance revealed that as it moved closer it lost some of its intensity, changing from a foreboding black to a steel grey. Not so ominous, Merrin thought, but plenty of rain there if it cared to drop it.

One of the sheepdogs came panting up to her, curious, little more than a puppy. Remembering that they were not pets Merrin nevertheless spoke softly to him, extending her hand. The sharp, intelligent face was wary, but he sniffed politely, lavished a lick and probably would have stayed to make friends had he not been summoned back by an imperative whistle.

It was Blase on the horse, riding with his usual relaxed seat, so thoroughly at home on the animal that he looked as if he had been born in the saddle. Merrin looked her fill, remembering that he had once told her that he had ridden before he had walked. Her father, no mean rider himself, had remarked several times that he didn't think the horse existed that Blase couldn't manage. She had believed him then; even now, although she was considerably less impressionable, she found it difficult to conceive of a horse that could unseat him.

He had seen her, of course, but he made no move towards her, not even lifting his hand. His determination to ignore her stung, but she swallowed fiercely and set off across the short grass, heading back to the house on an angle which would cut out the lagoon.

Before she was half way there the first rain began to fall, a shower of lightly scudding drops that barely dampened her hair.

Blase came out of the study as she walked down the hall. 'Can I see you?' he asked, phrasing an order as a question.

She nodded, preceding him into the room. It had darkened considerably and the lights were on, warm against the bleakness outside.

'What's this about Ellis?'

She told him, coolly and without emotion.

'I see. There's nothing anyone can do?'

'No, just make sure he isn't disturbed. He'll sleep overnight and be fine tomorrow.'

He frowned, looking down at the letter he held in his hand. 'Does he often get them?'

'Three or four a year.'

'Unpleasant.' The hazel eyes moved up to her face, holding her still. 'Ah well, you'll have to hold the fort for him tonight.'

'Surely I'm no substitute for Ellis. If the McGregors are lion-hunters——'

'Which they are not,' Blaze returned crisply. 'They're an amusing couple who give good parties, and you weren't invited because there was no way they could ignore you. They want you to come. You liked them, didn't you?'

'Yes, of course.' She turned away so that he could no longer catch her expression, saying dully, 'I don't feel in the mood for a party, Blase. And I'm sure you'd rather go without me. Certainly Coralie would.'

A pause, a kind of waiting, watchful silence before he said lightly, 'Jealous, Merrin?'

She bit her lip to prevent the gasp from escaping. Too quickly, in a voice which was too acid, she retorted, 'Conceited, Blase? Why should I be jealous? You have nothing to give me, so how can I fear that someone will take something from me? That's what jealousy is, isn't it?'

'I don't know,' he answered, 'but I know what it does. It eats away at your guts, tormenting you until you want to kill the object of your jealousy, just to get rid of the pain. Have you ever felt jealousy like that, Merrin?'

The question was a bitter taunt that needed no answer, but she shook her head, horrified by the raw violence in his voice.

'No, I thought not.' He dropped the letter into a tray and leaned backwards against the heavy wooden desk, watching her. A nerve flicked in his jaw, the tiny movement drawing attention to the harsh line of his mouth. From beneath the fans of his lashes, long enough to be the envy of most women, the darkened dominance of his eyes took in the pure lines of Merrin's profile.

Blase smiled. 'You weren't worth it, that's the joke! Tell me, purely as a matter of interest, how long did it take your husband to coax you into his bed? It took me only a few minutes, if I remember correctly, but he was younger, wasn't he? Perhaps he took your pro-testations literally? Or, once he knew that you were no innocent, did he manage to get you there that much faster? You did tell me, didn't you, that he knew you were no virgin?'

The words clawed at Merrin's heart, each insult aimed to wound and poison there, how accurately he could not know. White to the lips, she lifted her head proudly, unable to hurt him back. She had read some-where that the most vulnerable area of a man's ego was his sexual prowess; she had not believed it then, but Blase's attitude forced her to accept the accuracy of the statement.

He believed she had betrayed him, and then betrayed him again when she married Paul, reinforcing his con-tempt. Perhaps, when all his contempt and scorn had been purged, when he had exorcised the devils of humiliation which whipped his pride, he might be able to forget the past, or at least relegate it to its proper place.

'No answer?' His smile hardened into ruthlessness. Merrin drew a deep breath. She knew that smile of old. Sure enough, as she moved to go, he leaned forward and took her wrist, very gently.

As always his touch fired her blood. She stood very still while tension crackled between them, as dangerous as lightning on a hilltop. If she tried to escape those lean fingers would enjoy crushing the bones in their grip.

'Merrin?' His voice was deep, roughened with an emotion she recognised.

'No!' she exclaimed, looking up in appeal.

'That's the devil of the whole business,' he told her almost conversationally, drawing her closer. His lids were lowered so that it was impossible to see what he was thinking, but the irony that twisted his mouth warned her of further unpleasantness. 'I wonder what I'd have to do to rid myself of this sickness?'

'Don't give in to it.' Merrin pulled back, trying desperately to keep her voice light and steady. If he unleashed another onslaught on her she didn't think she could bear it. Already she was too close, too aware of his strength and the unique scent of him. Hastily she turned her head, afraid to pull against that inexorable grip, biting her lip in case she gave her emotions away.

'Enjoy your walk along the beach?' His other hand came up to touch her cheek in a caress that sent a shudder through her body.

He knew, of course, and amusement gleamed beneath the heavy lashes, amusement spiced by excitement. Merrin's hand came to rest against the hard wall of his chest, fingers splayed. He held it there deliberately, smiling as his heartbeat began to pick up speed.

'Don't be an idiot,' she said half under her breath while his hand followed the tender lines of her face and mouth. 'Blase, this is madness!'

He laughed, and she lost her temper and bit his finger hard, hoping to draw blood. Defiance glittered in the gaze she lifted to his.

'You're rather fond of biting,' he said, so softly that she could barely hear him. 'It's something you must have learned since you left Blackrocks—I don't remember that you indulged in it before.'

'Let me go, *please*,' she whispered.

'Don't be silly. You want this——' his mouth swooped, touched the soft hollow at the base of her throat and stayed there, so that his words were like kisses against her skin. '—every bit as much as I do.'

He let her go, but before she could run his hands
caught her across the waist and dragged her with cruel
purpose against him so that she could feel just how
much he wanted her. She gasped, hitting at him, futile
blows for his hands moved to grasp her hips and press
her closer, and he smiled at the torment so clearly
revealed in her face.

At last she stood, still held in that hateful embrace,
every muscle and sinew of his legs and thighs im-
printed on her body. The calculated insult could not
prevent her from responding to him, and although she
stood with head bent so that he couldn't see her face
she knew that he knew exactly what he was doing to
her.

'You didn't tell me how you enjoyed your walk along
the beach,' he said coolly.

Merrin bit her lip. After a moment she said stiffly,
'Very much.'

He moved, resettling his weight back against the
desk, holding her so that the adjustment of every
muscle was felt. Colour flaked the pallor of her cheeks.
He could not have made his wish to humiliate her more
clear.

'Good. I'd have offered you a lift back to the homestead, but I didn't think you'd accept.'

He spoke the cool conventional words with an
underlying thread of derision, forcing her to accept the
fact that she could not escape him. For as long as he
cared to keep up this farce of a conversation she had to
accept his sensual domination of her body. She was
being degraded, and he enjoyed doing it.

'You were right.' Her voice was icy cold, clear and
crisp and contemptuous.

One hand left her hips, moved slowly up beneath
her shirt to her bra, the lean fingers playing with the
clip. He smiled at the involuntary glance of anger that
scorched across her face and asked with silky determination, 'Don't you like standing like this,
Merrin?'

'No, I *hate* it!' The words came explosively through gritted teeth. Any movement led to further intimacy, further excitement for him. Coins of colour sprang into her cheeks. She lifted her head and surveyed him, breathing deeply to control her temper, trying to ignore the movement of his hand on her back, the hungry need deep within her that her anger could not hide.

'I think you'd better give me your promise to come tonight,' he said blandly.

The catch to her bra sprang loose and he began to stroke the skin of her back, each sensuous caress moving closer and closer to her breasts.

'If I do will you let me go?'

'Yes.'

Merrin stared at him, searching his face for some sign of gentleness. There was nothing there, only a granite hardness and the leaping, exulting flame of passion. Whatever they had shared in the past was gone, leaving only this desire to hurt and maim, this man torn and driven by a lust he despised.

Her shoulders straightened. 'Very well,' she said dully. 'I'll come.'

'Good.'

CHAPTER SEVEN

SHEER bravado, a refusal to show that she was at all intimidated, led to Merrin's decision to wear the white dress she had bought in Auckland. At least, she thought grimly as she applied make-up, she was going to go under with every flag she possessed flying high and proud!!

Against her holiday tan the gown looked superb, the back plunging to reveal her smooth golden shoulders. A dream in finely pleated georgette, the skirt fell in a narrow body-skimming swirl from beneath the cape which formed the sleeves and fell from the deep square neckline, preventing the clinging material from emphasising her high breasts too blatantly.

With thin-heeled sandals and demure pearl earrings it looked superb. Possibly a trifle too formal, but Mrs McGregor, had worn a stunning embroidered caftan to Hope's dinner party so presumably she liked her guests to dress up too. Merrin sprayed herself with 'Je Reviens' perfume, flicked a curl into place and took down her black velvet cloak. If she had to go tonight at least no one would think that she still carried a torch for Blase, she decided.

Whatever his reason for insisting on her presence he was polite enough to her on the drive into Whangarei. If there was menace beneath the smooth controlled courtesy she chose to ignore it. She was almost certain that she knew why her presence was necessary to him. Bitterly disgusted with himself because the physical attraction between them was as strong as ever, he wanted to punish her for it, and because he knew that she ached for him as desperately as she ever had, the punishment was to watch him with Coralie.

Hardly reasonable, but then men in the grip of a

passion stronger than their will-power were often unreasonable, she thought, and remembered Paul. He had loved her and lost any hope of gaining her love in return because of a jealousy he could not control. Now Blase was intent on paying her back for what he saw as her betrayal six years ago.

She knew now that she had been foolish to run away from Blackrocks. Had she been older, possessing the strength of character the years had gained for her, she would have stayed and made him believe that Terry had lied. It was her weakness which had driven her from the station, not Blase's cruelty, just as it was weakness which had led to that doomed marriage.

Perhaps weakness was a sin. Blase certainly thought so, if his careless epitaph for his cousin had been an indication of his feelings. Merrin sighed, snuggling into the warmth of her cloak.

'Cold?' He hadn't taken his eyes from the road and he couldn't have felt her slight movement, for, held in as they both were by the safety belts, they sat too far away for touch, but he knew exactly what she did. 'I can turn the heater up, if you are.'

'No, thank you.' She peered through the windscreen at the road, frowning as her eyes tried to pick up landmarks through the heavy drizzle. 'Aren't we past the turn-off to the Allens' station?'

'Yes. Coralie is in Whangarei, at her aunt's place in Kamo. We pick her up from there.' A short pause before he resumed without expression, 'She's spending the night at Blackrocks.'

Merrin nodded, suddenly weary of the whole situation. She felt that only an idiot would have submitted to Blase's sexual harassment and agreed to go with him, and cursed herself for being that idiot. At least with Coralie in the car on the way home there would be nothing like that. And if she couldn't avoid them at the party then the six years she'd spent away had been wasted ones.

'What do you think the weather is going to do?' she asked.

'At this time of the year it can do anything, but there was plenty of rain in that cloud.' He gestured at the steady thickness outside. 'It will probably be raining much more heavily than this when we come home. I may decide to leave early if it does look like flooding.'

She nodded again. The road to Blackrocks was well maintained, but the bridges across the numerous creeks were small and old. Several were only wooden platforms with no sides, and when it rained heavily, as it did quite often in this subtropical climate, they flooded, blocking traffic for a few hours. Those who lived on country roads in Northland paid strict attention to the amount of rain which fell.

Still, although the sky was lowering and the atmosphere distinctly unfriendly it was still only a drizzle which was falling when they arrived at the outskirts of the city.

'I'll be back in a moment,' Blase told her as the Jaguar drew up outside a large modern house set in pleasant, fashionable gardens.

Merrin nodded, waited until the door closed behind him and then climbed out. It might ease Coralie's fury if she came out to find Merrin in the back seat.

She had barely settled herself in before the door opened again and Coralie appeared, laughing, her flushed, beautiful face lifted to Blase's in a sparkling, challenging look that disappeared with ludicrous swiftness when she saw Merrin.

'You didn't tell me she was coming,' she said angrily as Blase put her into the front seat. 'I thought she'd be going with Mr Kimber.'

Embarrassed by her bad manners, Merrin said quietly, 'Ellis has a migraine, unfortunately!'

'Unfortunately for me!' As the door closed and Blase moved around to his side Coralie turned, her face distorted, and spat out, 'Just watch it! You look as though butter wouldn't melt in your mouth, but if you think you can get Blase back, forget it! He *despises* you.'

Tell me something new, Merrin thought, but Blase's arrival behind the wheel prevented any reply. Instantaneously Coralie turned, the spite and chagrin wiped from her expression as she favoured him with a wide sunny smile and a lighthearted comment on how magnificent he looked.

Not so childish, decided Merrin pensively. The seeming immaturity was, perhaps, a cloak to hide a basic greed and selfishness. She had been quick enough to pick up the vibrations between Blase and Merrin and appreciate the threat they constituted to her. If only she knew!

The party was a success. Held in a house of uncompromising modernity to the point of starkness, it ebbed and flowed in a flux of noise which started off as conversation but soon developed into the kind of joyous extravagance of pleasure only attained rarely. At some stage Merrin glanced at a piece of equipment which turned out to be a clock, deciphered the time and found to her intense astonishment that she was enjoying herself. The fact that the McGregors served only champagne possibly had some effect on her, but she had watched her intake carefully, so some other reason had to be found for this sudden upwelling of pleasure.

Possibly masculine attention, she thought drily, smiling at a question from one of the three men who were competing for her attention.

'I don't know,' she replied. 'My boss is having a lovely time, and shows no sign of wanting to move, so I suppose we're here until Blase throws us out.'

'He wouldn't be so cruel,' a redhaired man whose name was John said extravagantly. 'More likely to steal you for himself.'

'Hardly,' she returned without thinking, her eyes taking in a certain pair of broad shoulders across the room. Coralie was there too, clinging, her hands meeting across his forearm as if she was shackled there.

The oldest of Merrin's fans grinned cynically as he followed her glance. 'Oh, she's trying, but can you imagine it? She's a kid—and let's face it, Blase is very much a man. I know the Allens are dead keen—who wouldn't be?—but if I were a betting man, which I'm not, I'd give odds against.'

There came a snort of laughter from John, echoed by the third man, who said with hard amusement, 'You'd bet on the size of someone's socks. Still, I'm inclined to agree with you. Stanhope has a very avuncular air towards the delicious Coralie which must annoy her immensely.'

Remembering a certain embrace she had inadvertantly seen, Merrin couldn't agree, and found herself shocked at a certain warmth which made itself felt in her heart. So, whatever Hope and Moira Fieldgate might have said, it was by no means a certain thing in the district. And, she thought, the district gossip had a habit of being uncannily accurate.

Then, shocked by her lack of willpower where Blase was concerned, she allowed herself to be taken off by John to another room where the latest disco music was blaring.

It was apparent that John rather fancied his prowess as a dancer. After a few moments of selfconsciousness Merrin laughed suddenly and threw off her inhibitions, her black hair catching the light as she matched his movements.

'Hey,' he crowed, 'you are really something! Let's show this lot how it's done.'

Somebody began to clap in time to the music. Merrin felt the soft material of her skirt cling momentarily around her legs as she whirled, conscious through the heavy driving beat that people were moving back, stopping to watch them in a circle of smiling, absorbed faces as they left the floor clear for them.

Something pagan deep within Merrin stirred. She laughed again, her neat small features flushed, excitement lighting her eyes to emeralds as her feet and legs moved beneath a body made for rhythm. The music flowed through her, finding its perfect expression in her response to it. As long as she danced no other thought or emotion could intrude.

At last it ended, and she came back to earth to find herself and her partner the centre of an admiring circle which had been augmented by quite a few from the next room.

'Where did you learn to do that?' John exclaimed, astonished, laughing, his fair skin flushed with exertion as he put a proprietorial hand on her arm. He was breathing heavily and his touch on her skin was warm and damp.

Merrin was uncomfortable. One of the penalties of loving Blase was a physical unease at the touch of another man, but she suffered it to remain there, aware that John meant nothing by it. He was merely expressing his delight at having found a partner worthy of him. Perhaps even better than he was, certainly very dramatic with her vivid colouring, her eyes like enormous green jewels in her small face, the soft whiteness of her dress stark against the smooth gold shoulders and arms.

'Hey, how about this?' he asked, as somebody put on a moody romantic air, very suitable for winding down to.

'Sorry, but this is mine.' Blase's voice was cool, but some note in the deep tones made John flush vividly and step back, suddenly on edge.

Merrin's whole body contracted. She could not bear—*would* not bear Blase's hold. 'I'm so thirsty,' she said, forcing the words to come lightly as she turned slightly to meet the implacable depths of his glance.

He smiled, handed her a glass of champagne and without saying a word made the younger man realise that he was totally superfluous. Merrin bit her lip, furious as John stammered his thanks and moved on. How did Blase do it? Superb arrogance, she thought, refusing to meet his eyes as she sipped the cool golden liquid.

The end of the disco record had left her and her partner in the centre of the floor. They had not moved, but with the advent of the next tape others had taken the empty floor so that she and Blase stood among dancers, so still that they might have been statues, held in that small globe of stillness. The lighting was so subdued that it was difficult to see anything more than the pale glimmer of shirt fronts and those few women's dresses in light colours.

The columns of champagne bubbles wavered as Merrin's hand trembled; she looked up and said softly, 'I'm tired.'

He smiled and took her in his arms, moving with sensuous grace. Merrin held the glass between them, determined not to spill it. His hands moved to her shoulders, steering her through the dancers to a table where he took the glass and placed it before drawing her fully within the circle of his arms.

The temptation to rest her head against his shoulder was almost irresistible. A shudder of desire shook her momentarily. His hold tightened, so that she was brought up against him, taut against his hard strength. The music flowed past them, seducingly sweet with a touch of wry sophistication and Merrin responded as she always had, swaying gracefully, small and fragile against his lean strength. His head bent, came to rest on the soft waves in a movement which in any other man would have been tenderness. Every muscle in her body tightened in an agony of rejection.

'What are you doing?' she asked huskily.

'Making a point.' His voice was deep, almost without emotion. Merrin turned her head, almost stifled by the intense sexual aura he was enveloping her in. Across the room she met Coralie's eyes and saw in them anger and a kind of shocked bewilderment. Anger refuelled her contempt. Thinly she snapped, 'If Coralie is supposed to be on the receiving end you can stop it now. She's got the message.'

'You sound very disdainful.'

She felt the movement of his cheek as he smiled and could imagine that smile, mocking, cold with an amusement which denied itself.

'I don't like what you're doing to her,' she said, scorn sharpening the words into an accusation.

'And what am I doing to her?'

The tone of his voice should have warned her to be silent, but Merrin threw back her head to look fearlessly into his eyes, her own very direct and level. 'Teaching her a lesson, perhaps?'

His hand came up, touched her cheek in a gesture which must have seemed affectionate, even loving. Only Merrin could see the unholy appreciation which lit the gold-green depths as he smiled down at her. 'Exactly,' he told her with cold insolence.

'And you're very good at that.' The words fell between them, heavy with memories.

A muscle flicked against the hard jaw. Shutters fell; Blase's expression became withdrawn, the splendid bone structure a mask to hide his thoughts. But his hands tightened, holding her to him.

'We're two of a kind, you and I,' he agreed, relaxing that cruel grip as the music swelled to a climax. 'Your lessons are pointed, carefully chosen to wound and maim. Do you think I should marry Coralie?'

The unexpectedness of the question shocked her. She turned her head away, saying in a muffled voice, 'I wouldn't wish you on my worst enemy.'

'And she's not that, merely a child who's suffering from an adolescent crush.' He laughed, deep in his throat, tipping her chin so that her face was tilted towards him. From beneath his lashes his glance raked the small, pointed oval, lingering with insolent sensuality on her mouth, and from then dropping to where her breasts rose, high and smoothly golden, before the white material of her dress hid them from a glance as bold as his.

'You'd like to hit me,' he murmured, correctly assessing her reaction, 'but don't. I'll hit you back, and although the McGregors like to think of themselves as madly up-to-date, I doubt if they'd be able to cope with that.' His fingers curled around her throat, cutting off her breath, then relaxed and moved to her waist again. 'So you don't think I should put Coralie out of her misery? I wonder who would suffer most if I did, she or I?'

'She would.' Merrin lifted a gaze glittering with defiance. 'Can you suffer? You seem to be totally impregnable. Emotionally, I mean, not physically.'

He bent his head so that his breath played across her mouth as he spoke. 'I suffered once, Merrin, believe me. And I vowed then that I'd never let myself get in a situation like that again. Only a fool goes about offering hostages to the gods, refusing to learn from his mistakes. Don't you agree?'

'I couldn't agree more,' she said tiredly, exhausted by the control needed to prevent herself from melting against him in open invitation.

'Then we know exactly where we are,' he returned with satisfaction, and smiled down into her expressionless face as the tape came to its end.

He relinquished her into John's care with such suave self-possession that she felt like kicking him. Indeed, if she hadn't been convinced that he would be able to cope superbly with such a mannerless gesture she might have forgotten every precept of behaviour drummed into her by her mother and done just that.

It was pleasant to be in John's undemanding company. He was curious, as everyone must be, about her exact relationship to Blase and because he made no effort to satisfy that curiosity she took pity on him and told him of her years spent at Blackrocks.

'So you and Blase are old friends,' he said, nodding.

'From the time I was twelve,' she replied a little drily.

'Ah, that explains it.' He grinned as she lifted her brows at him. 'Well, you seem thoroughly at home with him. Like the two halves of a whole.' A look of astonishment crossed his features. 'Um, I suppose that's not right either; it sort of implies something more than friendship.'

'Listen to that rain,' she said vaguely, turning her head to look at the curtains which hid the night.

Sure enough, five minutes later Blase came across with a purposeful frown between his brows. 'Sorry,' he said, clearly lying, 'but I think it's time to say goodbye, Merrin. I've rung home and Hope says it's been raining steadily there for some hours.'

Merrin nodded. 'I'll get my cloak.'

Coralie was in the bedroom collecting her wrap. She looked up as the door opened, and said harshly, 'I hope you've enjoyed yourself tonight!'

'In places.' Merrin yawned, feeling profoundly sorry for the girl, and extremely cross with Blase.

Fortunately Mrs McGregor came in then, and within a few minutes they were in the Jaguar, heading through the rain, by now a torrential downpour. For almost half of the way home there was silence until an immense clap of thunder startled them all.

'We shouldn't have left!' Coralie's voice was highpitched enough to reach the back of the car. 'Blase, can't we go back? We'll never make it to Blackrocks.'

'We won't make it back, either. This is a cloudburst, honey, and the creek is nearly across the road now. It will be localised, probably just in the hills. Almost certainly it'll ease off once we get over the summit.'

She reacted to the reassurance of his tones with a stifled sob. 'But the creeks will all be flooded up there too! We'll be stranded.'

'I can think of worse things than being stranded for the rest of the night with you.'

Merrin stiffened at the lazy note of mockery in the deep tones, angry with him for so blatantly using his sexuality to charm the girl from her fears.

As if he had seen the quick involuntary movement of her hands he raised his voice slightly, pitching it to the back of the car. 'How about you, Merrin? O.K.?'

'Fine. I think you're right. Once we're on to Blackrocks the rain will almost certainly ease up.'

'There you are, Coralie. Calm down now, we'll get you home safe and sound. Have I ever let you down?'

'No.' But Coralie huddled back into the seat, her fear tangible and oppressive.

Merrin felt sorry for her, and cursed her inconvenient emotion. It would be much easier if she could hate the younger girl, but she could only feel this profound debilitating sympathy. In one way she was right. It was dangerous to be driving in such an intense downpour, especially on this narrow gravel road. But it would be more dangerous to stop, for here the road followed the creek and soon the water would be across the road. Even on Blackrocks hill, above flood level, they would not be able to stop, for there was always the possibility of a landslide. Northland's soils were notoriously unstable where the protective cover of bush had been removed and there had been many occasions when the road had been closed by slips. They would be safe only when they had crossed the hills and could stop on land above flood level on Blackrocks.

If anyone could get them through it would be Blase. Not only did he know every stone and pothole on the road, but he was as skilful at driving as he was at everything else, his eyesight perfect, his reactions hair-trigger.

Relaxation would not come, of course, but Merrin sat almost at ease behind him, her eyes fixed on his silhouette against the muted glow of the headlights while outside the rain fell in solid sheets, almost beating the efforts of the wipers to clear it from the windscreen. Coralie crouched against the seat, staring at him, her profile sharpened by fear. Once she said something, but the rain was too heavy for the words to be clear and when Blase answered it was with an abruptness that forced her to relapse back into silence.

The road up the side of the hill seemed never-

ending, but Blase handled the conditions superbly.
When they reached the top Merrin's sigh of relief came
softly through her stiff lips even though she knew that
in some ways it was more dangerous to descend than
to climb.

True to his prophecy, the rain eased, but so slightly
that there could be no prospect of getting home
tonight. The creeks in the flats below would be well
over their banks. The safest thing to do would be to
make for Appleton's homestead, about half a mile past
the turning to Blackrocks, and spend the night there.
Merrin searched her memory. She was almost certain
that the road crossed no creeks in that short distance,
and Mrs Appleton was the sort of capable housewife
who wouldn't be flustered by the unexpected arrival of
three people in the middle of the night. No doubt Blase
had already decided on this. At the moment he was
skilfully coaxing the car down a road which was a dangerous clay slick more closely resembling a river bed
every long moment which went past.

Then their luck ran out. Above the noise of the rain
a lower, deeper grumble reverberated through the car.
As the mass of mud and stone came hurtling down
Coralie screamed, grabbing the wheel so that the car
slewed. Blase shouted something but made only the
smallest attempt to duck when a stone bounced from
the road up through the windscreen. A fraction of a
second later pain exploded in Merrin's head.

The first sound she heard was sobbing, high-
pitched, hysterical sobbing which almost drowned out
the heavy thrumming of the rain. It sawed through her
head, setting off a million agonising pains, scrambling
her thoughts so that she could only lie against the seat
wishing that it would go away. After long moments
the sound resolved itself into Coralie's voice, harsh and
high-pitched, calling Blase's name over and over again.
Merrin opened her eyes to complete darkness. After
more endless moments she could just make out the
girl's silhouette bending over a formless hump which

could only be Blase.

'Stop shaking him!' How she managed to summon up the words Merrin didn't know. Her voice was thick and wavering, but at least it attracted Coralie's attention.

'He's dead!' she screamed, and collapsed, her terror rocketing up into panic.

Wincing, Merrin hauled herself forward, grabbed the girl's shoulders and shook her ferociously. 'Shut up!' she jerked.

The rain threatened the silence; Coralie relapsed into choked whimpers. With one hand to her exploding head Merrin felt cautiously with the other for a pulse in the hollow beneath Blase's ear, found it and only then realised that she had been holding her breath.

'He's alive,' she said roughly, grabbing Coralie's hand and guiding it to where that signal of existence beat strong and slow. 'He's just been knocked out.'

Coralie jerked her hand away. 'There's blood on his head!' The words were shrill, barely recognisable. Obviously she was in the grip of terror beyond reason. Merrin felt the familiar exasperated sympathy well up within her, but knew that she could not give way to it. If they were to get out of this without too much damage Coralie was going to have to regain control of herself, and the sooner the better.

'You must have seen it before,' she snapped. 'Did you turn the car off?'

'No.'

It took all Merrin's strength to lean across the seat and turn the key off and when it was done she wasn't even sure why she felt impelled to do it. Then she tried the interior light, but it failed. 'A torch,' she said slowly, out loud, because she could not think with the pain in her head. 'There should be a torch. Find it.'

A few moments later the shrill young voice said, 'Here it is. Don't—I won't look at him! I won't! I won't!'

'Shut up, or I'll hit you!' Merrin drew a deep breath,

forcing herself to concentrate. 'Can you climb over into the back?'

'Yes.' Followed a flurry of movement and then Coralie whispered from beside her, 'I hate blood. I can't bear it.'

'All right.' Merrin moved experimentally. Her head seemed twice its normal size and her neck and shoulders ached, but there was nothing else wrong with her. 'Undo my zip,' she ordered. 'I'm going over to the front and it will be a lot easier if I'm out of this dress.'

Silence as fingers fumbled, found the zip and pulled it down. As she wriggled free of the clinging material the coppery taste of nausea thickened in Merrin's throat, but she finally rested against the seat, naked except for her bra and pants.

'Now, I'll probably need a push over,' she said thickly.

Once in the front seat she had to stay still for some minutes, fighting down the sickness that threatened. While she lay against the seat Coralie called out her name, the fear in her voice making it only too clear just how tenuous a hold the younger girl had on her self-control.

'It's O.K.,' Merrin whispered tiredly.

'I thought—I thought you were both dead.'

'No. We're very much alive.' Merrin licked her lips. 'Blase is as tough as old boots, you know that. And he said he'd get you home. He will.'

'It sounds as though you will,' Coralie whimpered, making a brave effort at normality. 'You're like him, aren't you?'

'Tough—as old boots?'

'No. Reliable.'

'Oh, we try.' The sickness receded. Merrin picked up the torch and directed it at Blase, and her breath caught in her throat. The rock had hit him on the side of his head, fortunately avoiding the temple, but a sharp edge had split the skin so that blood and mud oozed in a ghastly mixture clotting the dark honey hair.

He had been knocked back into the door and lay with rain from the broken window beating on to his chest, his expression empty of the driving vitality which was so dominant a characteristic.

Somewhere, Merrin thought slowly, there should be a first aid box. All of the Blackrock vehicles had medical supplies in them. By now the pain in her head had settled down into a steady splitting ache that zagged through her skull every time she moved it, but she found the box, took out the scissors and by dint of speaking sharply to Coralie, managed to force her to hold the torch while she cut the hair from around the wound.

Greatly encouraged by the fact that this caused his brows to twitch together, she said, 'Here, hold this cloth out of the window.'

It took time to clean the blow. She had to pause several times to fight back the nausea which assailed her and once she had such a bout of shivering that her hands couldn't obey her, but at last it lay clean. It was nasty, but like her Blase had only been struck a glancing blow. Surely, she thought hopefully, there could be no possibility of a fracture of the skull?

Biting her lips to control the pang of fear she could not entirely suppress, she shook antibiotic powder on to the now sluggishly bleeding wound just as he opened his eyes.

'Sh,' she said automatically. 'We're all right.'

The torch was still aimed at the wound; he frowned, closing his eyes against the light.

'Coralie?'

'She's fine. Don't worry. You've had a bang on the head, but it takes more than a stray boulder to do much damage to you.'

The hard mouth lifted at the corners. 'And you?'

'Oh, you can't kill a weed.' She was not going to tell him about the blow she had received. He had enough to worry him.

The eyes opened, rested on her absorbed intent face

with surprising shrewdness. One hand lifted, touched her bare waist and lingered there. 'Naked ministering angels?' he muttered, the mockery back.

Heartened, Merrin smiled and sat back. 'The very latest thing in angels. Coralie, pass me something to block this window with, will you?'

The something was her cloak. Merrin said swiftly, 'No, the dress, I think. I'm going to need this.'

Blase moved as she carefully stuffed her beautiful white dress into the surprisingly small hole left by the rock. They had been lucky. Had the wretched thing been any larger it could well have killed him, if not her.

'You can't do anything,' she said severely as a short hissing breath told her of the pain his unguarded movement had caused him. 'Just lie still.'

He had relapsed back into unconsciousness, the fine features blank in the pallor of his skin. 'Turn the torch off,' Merrin said harshly. 'Someone is going to need it when they go for help.'

'No!' Coralie began to weep again. 'I can't! You can't make me! I'm terrified of the dark—you know I am. Blase, tell her I've always been afraid of the dark.' Her voice began to rise, became shriller as she lost her hold on reality. 'It's a phobia——'

There was only one way this could end. Fortunately Merrin's hand found the soft cheek the first time. At the resounding slap she delivered Coralie gasped and gulped, then began to sob, harsh rigours shaking her slender shoulders. 'I won't let you leave me,' she whimpered. 'We'll all stay here. Wait until the morning. You're not to go.'

Merrin's patience snapped. 'Listen to me, you selfish little girl, and listen well.' Her voice was low and harsh, pitched so that it could only just be heard above the still heavy thunder and the rain on the roof. 'I don't give a darn about you, or your phobias, or your precious little self. Quite frankly, I find you entirely superfluous. But Blase needs help, and I'm going to

see that he gets it. You can do one of two things—walk
the half mile to the Appletons' place, or stay here with
him. Make up your mind which it's to be.'

Silence, and then, 'How *dare* you!' in tones quivering
with fury proved that the combination of pain and
plain speaking had driven away the incipient hysteria.

'Oh, with ease,' Merrin said grimly.

'Because you're in love with him. Did you think I
hadn't noticed? It's so obvious that everyone knows.
You're a laughing stock——'

'Do you want another slap?'

The ice in Merrin's voice effectively silenced the
younger girl. More gently Merrin continued, 'If you're
going to be any help to him you must try to control
yourself so that when he recovers consciousness you
can give him some of your strength. Now, pass me the
rug in the back.'

'But I'm using it.'

'Blase needs it more than you do.'

There was silence, but then Coralie muttered as she
handed the rug across, 'I'm sorry.'

'That's O.K.' Merrin tucked the rug around his
form, stilled as she felt him move and impelled by an
impulse she could no longer resist kissed him lightly
on the brow. It would be the last time she ever kissed
him, the last time she could do anything for him, and
she knew a fierce joy that she was able to give him
something more than the temporary solace of her
body.

Beneath her lips his head moved, so softly that she
could barely hear the words he said, 'You are not . . .
not to go.' And when she made no reply, 'Merrin? Did
you hear . . .?'

'Yes, I heard. Lie still now, my love. Go back to
sleep.'

'Bloody . . . head . . .' His head moved against her
arm. She felt his mouth cling to her shoulder and
before she broke down completely said crisply, 'You'd
better climb back into the front when I've gone,

Coralie, so that you can keep an eye on him.'

'Is he—is he all right? Not bleeding?'

'No. The bleeding's stopped.'

The little voice from the back became fretful, almost petulant. 'It's cold!'

'Cuddle up to Blase. It will keep you both warm.' Merrin had to pause a moment as her head was thumping unbearably. Then she began to dress, hauling on her wrap over her bra and pants.

It seemed hours later that she was leaving the car clad in oilskins she had found in the trunk, an umbrella in one hand, the torch in the other. She had already placed a warning cone behind the car; the other was tucked under her arm. By now she was very cold, shivering almost continually as she picked her way across the debris of the slip. It had been only a small one, mainly mud with a few biggish boulders and some trees tangled up in it. Ten minutes' work with a bulldozer would see the road clear enough for one-way traffic to resume.

Just sheer bad luck, she thought, pushing to the back of her mind the question of how much damage Coralie's panic-stricken grab at the wheel had done. Highly strung child that she was, it was too much to expect from her the kind of control it had taken Merrin six hard years to acquire. Blase, of course, had been born with it; no doubt he could afford to ignore Coralie's hysterical tendencies when she had so much else to offer him.

Blinking fiercely, Merrin stooped to place the second cone on the far side of the slip. As she straightened she took a deep breath, her hand pressing for a moment against her head. The blood which had seeped into her hair had dried and become matted and the pain there had dulled; even the ache inside it was less now, possibly because of the fresh air, possibly because she knew that she had to get help for Blase.

CHAPTER EIGHT

In after years Merrin could never remember much of the nightmare trek down the hill and along to Appleton's homestead, only that she had done quite a bit of it by whispering his name over and over as she lifted each heavy foot. Dazed, almost entranced by her ordeal, she went a few paces past the white letter box at their gate. It was this forced retracing of her steps which made her cry; the hundred yards or so up to the house seemed like half a world away.

One of the dogs began to bark, the deep gruff noise penetrating the thunder and the rattle of the rain on to the roof of the implement shed.

Before Merrin had made it to the back door there was someone there, torch in hand, calling urgently for a lamp to be lit as the power had gone off.

After that there was more noise but no confusion as Mr Appleton and his four large sons set off into the night and Merrin was put, shivering, into a warm bath under Mrs Appleton's clear blue gaze.

'Shock,' that lady observed sapiently, as Merrin made some attempt to wipe away the tears which ran down her face. 'And that thump on your head won't have helped, either. Now, don't worry! Greg has taken the bulldozer and the others are in the Land Rover, so they'll be able to clear a way through the slip and bring Blase and Coralie back. And in the morning you and he can both get your heads X-rayed at Whangarei just to make sure there's nothing wrong with either of you.'

She was large and comfortable and thirty years ago she had been a nurse, so when she finally ordered Merrin out of the bath and proceeded to dry her down Merrin relaxed, taken back to the childhood security represented by a warm bath and a towel.

'This will be far too large for you, but at least it's warm,' her hostess said, dropping a blue nightgown over her head. 'Now, get into that dressing gown and come into the kitchen and I'll see to that cut.'

The kitchen was big, warm from the enormous wood range in one wall. Hurricane lamps cast a warm glow over immaculate paintwork and all the latest appliances, useless now until the power was restored, but the heart of the house still functioned. An ember clinked against the grate as Mrs Appleton dropped in a tea-tree log.

'Quite a few people got rid of their wood ranges when the power came through,' she said comfortably, setting a kettle on to the element, 'but I've never regretted keeping ours.'

'Blackrocks still has theirs too.'

'Yes. Moira Fieldgate swears by it for breadmaking.' She caught up a bowl reeking with the sharp scent of disinfectant. 'Let's have a look, shall we? Hmm, you were lucky, it's just a graze. I won't cut any hair away, just bathe it. You won't need stitches.'

Tears came again to Merrin's eyes. She looked down at her hands, clenched them tight. 'I had to cut Blase's hair. His—his head is cut. The rock hit him first. He—he couldn't even shield himself with his arm.'

Because Coralie had grabbed the wheel and he needed both hands to see that they didn't go over the edge into the valley below. He could have ducked further; indeed, he had begun to move, instinctively flinching away from the threat, but for some reason he had not followed through and he had been hit, God knew how hard.

'He'll be all right,' Mrs Appleton told her soothingly. 'You couldn't kill Blase—he's a survivor. So are you, I'd say. That was a long walk to do in the pitch dark with a bump the size of an egg on your head. How's the headache?'

'Bloody awful!'

Mrs Appleton chuckled, but laid a cool hand on her forehead. 'You were knocked unconscious, weren't you? You're probably very slightly concussed. Have you been sick?'

'No, although I've felt like it a couple of times.'

'You'll be all right.' She pulled the hissing kettle to one side. 'I'll heat you some milk and then you can get into bed.'

'No!' At the older woman's shrewd, surprised look Merrin flushed but said, 'I'll wait up until they get back. I—I want to make sure he's all right.'

'Was there any bleeding from his ears or his mouth?'

Merrin shook her head. 'No, not that I could see. Not from his mouth anyway.'

'No depression in the skull?'

'No.'

'Then it's not likely to be fractured, if that's what you're worrying about. If I know Blase he'll come in on his feet, furious with you for going out into that rain and about as co-operative as a shark in a feeding frenzy!'

Her companion's use of imagery made Merrin chuckle, but she sat stubbornly by the fire and sipped her milk, refusing to leave the big, cheerful room even though her lashes continually fell to cover eyes which were gritty and aching.

At last, through the rumble of the now distant thunder and the relentless tattoo of the rain came the sound of an engine labouring up the drive.

'Stay there!' Mrs Appleton ordered, moving with a speed surprising in a woman of her build.

Coralie came first, white with exhaustion as she clung to Dave Appleton's arm. Then Blase, also pale and very grim about the mouth. When his glance fell on Merrin, small in the tent of her hostess's dressing gown, something flared to life in his eyes. He took a step away from Tom's supporting arm, but almost immediately swayed and swore, luridly and with a total disregard for the feminine members of the party.

'*Conscience avaunt, Richard's himself again*,' Merrin quoted shakily, relief making her frivolous.

Everyone but Blase stared at her; he scowled and then grinned. 'Well, having your head stove in doesn't seem to have done you any harm. Let me have a look.'

It was obvious that he wasn't going to move until she had shown him, so she rose and made her way across the room to stand in front of him, head slightly bent so that he could see for himself. His hand came up, pushed a strand of hair back and very gently, traced the path of the rock across her scalp.

'Obviously a head like concrete,' he jeered, and then, half beneath his breath, 'Thank you.'

Shrilly, almost shocking in the silence, Coralie said, 'Hadn't you better get to bed, Blase? You look like death!'

Merrin moved, caught her foot in the voluminous folds of Mrs Appleton's dressing gown and tripped. Head thumping crazily, she was caught, held for a moment against his lean frame, before Blase said abruptly, 'You couldn't be more right, Coralie.'

As Merrin stepped away he smiled at his hostess, using that charm he so unfairly possessed. 'But I'll bet you're going to use me to polish up on your old skills.'

Mrs Appleton smiled. 'Yes, I'll have a look at it. However, it can wait until I've shown Merrin where she's going to spend what's left of the night. Come on, young lady, you're asleep on your feet.'

The bed was warmed by three hot water bottles. Merrin felt only the covers go over her body before she sank into a sleep so deep that nothing woke her, not Coralie's subsequent arrival in the other of the twin beds, not the bustle of a big and busy household around her, until the sound of a helicopter swooping low over the house penetrated the mists.

'Well, sleeping beauty! Come on, it's time for you to get going. That chopper is here to take you and Blase across the hill to Whangarei.'

Mrs Appleton was as cheerful and vital as if she hadn't spent a good proportion of the night awake and busy. Setting a tray down on the bedside table, she continued, 'How's your head?'

Merrin lifted it experimentally from the pillow. 'Fine,' she answered somewhat disbelievingly. 'Very slightly achy and my neck is a bit stiff, but otherwise O.K. How's Blase?'

'Bad-tempered and itching to get out. Fortunately there's been very little damage to Blackrocks, so he isn't desperate. I don't have to tell you that if he thought his precious station needed him he'd be in, boots and all, and no worry about his head. Men! Now, drink this tea and then I'll bring in some clothes. I've managed to rake up some of Sally's clobber, so you'll have things that fit you better than that nightgown.'

Sally was her daughter, now nursing, but fortunately she had left behind jeans and a tee-shirt which were not more than a size too big for Merrin.

'You look like a refugee,' Coralie commented, drifting into the room when Merrin had dressed. Obviously she had been at Sally's clobber first. 'Mrs Appleton, I'll make breakfast for the boys, shall I? It must be time for them to get back.'

'Better wait until we see them,' her hostess told her practically. 'Come on, Merrin. The pilot must be just about on his way back. He's been checking damage. Tom says there are fences and bridges down all over and several log jams on the creeks, but we've been lucky. It could have been worse. Eight inches in six hours, we had.'

Blase was already out in the paddock with Tom; he was leaning against a gate post as he watched the helicopter come swooping in over the paddock and settle down gently on its skids.

'Come on,' he mouthed at her, warning her with a gesture to duck her head because the blades were still turning. He looked tired, a little drawn, the slashes in his cheeks more strongly emphasised by the bright sunlight.

Merrin's heart was wrung with a kind of anguish which held her still and frozen during the trip to the hospital. For the first time she faced the fact that what was between them was more than the driving physical hunger she had assumed it to be. Oh, that was part of it, this need which hurt at times with the painful excitement only he aroused in her, but there was much more to it than that. Reduced to its simplest and loveliest terms, she loved him. Incredible, to lose your heart to a man when you were twelve and he eighteen, to love after the cruellest betrayal and through all the empty years and still to love, hopelessly and without any limits.

A bitter smile touched her lips. Surely she must hold some sort of record for fidelity! Had Patient Griselda felt this compound of pain and humiliation at her lack of willpower? Certainly it was not because she wanted to love him. Only a masochist could enjoy this shameful dependence on someone who cared nothing for her beyond desiring her as a convenient outlet for his passion.

I must be conditioned to it, she thought wearily, staring sightlessly down at the lush farmlands spread out like a map below. Conditioned by an adolescence spent within his orbit; in her most impressionable years she had grown to think of him as the only stable influence in her life. Even at fourteen his touch had excited her, but she had loved him for years before that, long before the terrifying turmoil in her body had been eased by him in the only way that mattered.

His hand on her cheek startled her from her thoughts. She looked up, met the green-gold of his regard and smiled, for he looked concerned. The lean fingers trembled slightly against her skin, but that was merely the first sign that they were over Whangarei and coming in to land, for simultaneously the engine note changed as the machine lurched. It took all her strength to subdue her desire to burn her mouth into the palm of his hand, but she managed it. And then Blase took her hand and held it until they were down and the pilot jumped out to help her, swinging her on to the ground with a smile and an unheard quip.

Blase disdained any support but put his arm around her as they ran beneath the fiercely beating rotors to where a small group of people waited.

Before they had reached the group a flash flared and Blase swore. One of the men who waited was a doctor, but the other had to be a reporter.

'Do you want to be a heroine?' Blase asked, snapping the words viciously into her ear.

Merrin shook her head, her eyes searching his face. Of course, if anyone got to know of that nightmare walk last night Coralie could be made to feel more embarrassed than she already was about her phobia. He was sheltering her.

'Then shut up and don't say anything to anyone.'

It was the heat, and perhaps she was still exhausted, but as they reached those who waited Merrin stumbled. After that it was easy. She and Blase were bundled into the hospital, where a Sister joked with Blase as she took their particulars. The reporter had to wait outside.

Nothing hurried the steady routine of the hospital, not even Blase's chafing impatience to be gone, but at last the X-rays were checked and the doctor told them that they were lucky, no signs of any fracture in either skull.

'But we're keeping you here for twenty-four hours,' he told Merrin firmly. 'You need some rest, and Mr Stanhope tells me you'll not get any out at Blackrocks.'

Merrin met the hard glitter of Blase's eyes and realised that it was his idea that she should stay. Pain made her lips tighten, pain and anger. He couldn't have made his indifference to her more clear.

'How are you getting back?' she asked huskily.

'Same way as we came.' He looked down at her, frowning. 'O.K.?'

She nodded, not trusting herself to say anything else. The tension must have been obvious, for the doctor said quietly, 'The nurse will show you to the ward, Miss—Mrs Sinclair.'

And that was that. Wherever the reporter lurked it wasn't in the ward, so that he had no chance to badger her for any details of the experience. Possibly as well as the painkillers they gave her a sedative, because she slept for most of the day and soundly, heavily, during the night, to wake to another glorious morning.

'There you are,' one of the nurses said, handing her a newspaper. 'Lucky you! I'd break my leg if it would get Blase Stanhope to put his arm around me!'

Sure enough, in the photograph they looked like lovers, he protective, almost tender as he looked down at her, she suitably submissive.

'How to deceive the eye,' she murmured, her expression remote as she read the caption and the small news article that went with it.

Blase had been incredibly discreet. To anyone not familiar with the road it sounded as though the slip had hit them only a few yards from Appleton's homestead. There was nothing about her expedition through the storm at all, which was exactly as she wanted things to be. No heroine stuff, no mention of Coralie.

'Thank you,' she murmured, handing the newspaper back.

'Oh, you keep it.' The young nurse twinkled down at Merrin. 'You might want to keep the photo for a souvenir. He's gorgeous, isn't he? Like the very sexiest sort of film star. I suppose he's just an ordinary man behind those fabulous looks.'

'Not entirely.' Merrin's voice was dry enough to attract the nurse's slightly puzzled glance for a moment. Hastily she added, 'He's got more than his looks. In fact, when you meet him you tend to forget about them.'

The nurse nodded knowingly. 'Charisma, that is. Lucky man. Why hasn't he got married?'

Merrin managed a smile, tolerant but uninterested. 'I don't know him well enough to ask him.'

'Pity.' The nurse looked regretful, but cheered up to say, 'Well, you'll be out this morning, I hear. How are you getting back?'

'By road. It says here that they've put Bailey bridges across all of the washouts, so there'll be no problem.'

'You'll be glad to get out of here, I suppose.'

Merrin smiled, one hand touching the now barely perceptible bump on the side of her head. 'Yes, I'm afraid I will. You've all been very kind, but hospitals are not my favourite places.'

'Not anybody's, so don't look so guilty. Well, you've seen the North at its worst; with any luck we'll have a good autumn from now on. How much longer are you planning to stay?'

Merrin didn't blame her for seeking information, it was a human and entirely understandable characteristic. Smiling, she returned an evasive answer and the girl soon left her. Shortly after that she was told by a doctor that she had been discharged and the Sister in charge of the ward handed her a case containing clothes—bra and pants, a narrow-skirted suit of pale blue and high, thin-heeled black shoes. A city outfit. When she had dressed Merrin looked at herself in the mirror and sighed.

Once she had been as outgoing as the young nurse, fresh and eager, her vitality at full flow. Now she looked older than her twenty-four years, the weariness in her eyes overshadowing the youthful cast of her features and the fine, smooth skin. Almost she looked defeated, as though life had won in a battle which had been fought with bloody hands.

Wearily she picked up the case and made her way through the ward.

To her intense astonishment it was Blase who waited for her, elegant in a dark suit, his hair gleaming in the sunlight as he talked to the Sister. As she came through the swing doors he looked up. There was a flare of emotion in the hazel eyes and then he smiled, and said something to the Sister before coming forward to take the case from Merrin's hand.

'You look good enough to eat,' he said, and in front of the Sister and one or two nurses who happened to be passing bent and kissed her lightly on the cheek.

Merrin couldn't help it. She flinched as he touched her, well aware that she had gone very pale.

Instantly his hand was at her waist, the cruel grip of his fingers reinforcing his possessive attitude.

'Careful, or they'll insist you spend another day here,' he said lightly, and the Sister smiled, her shrewd eyes knowing as they rested on Merrin's now rosy face.

'Oh, I don't think we'll do that. She really didn't need to be here at all, but I heard that someone insisted.' Her voice left no doubt as to what construction she put on that piece of high-handedness.

Merrin closed her eyes, angry and bewildered. For some reason Blase was going out of his way to stake a claim to her, and she shuddered to think what his devious brain had come up with now.

'Better sure than sorry,' he said now. Blase, who *never* spoke in clichés!—and then stage-managed her goodbyes and thanks so swiftly that Merrin found herself outside in the warm sunlight before she had a chance to think.

He saw her view Ellis's car with lifted brows and remarked with a rapid return to his normal sardonic tones, 'The Jag is still without a windscreen, so Ellis very kindly offered his.'

Involuntarily her eyes lifted to his head, searching for the spot where he had been hit.

'It's fine,' he told her brusquely.

'Why didn't you duck?' she asked tightly.

'I did. I just didn't react fast enough.'

Obstinately she shook her head. 'I'm not a fool,

Blase. You started to jerk away then you stopped. Why?'

He tossed the case into the back of the car, slammed the boot down with unnecessary force and came round to where she stood, pale but determined. His anger showed in the hard line of his jaw as he opened her door, saying curtly, 'Call it a chivalrous impulse. Now get in.'

So she had been right. He had deliberately gone against every instinct he possessed and offered himself as a sacrifice to protect her. An intolerable gratitude filled her.

As he started the motor she said quietly, 'Thank you——'

'I don't want gratitude.' He turned to see where he was reversing, his powerful shoulders taut against his coat, his expression forbidding. 'Look, just keep quiet for a while, will you? This car is still new to me.'

He was putting her off, of course; he had her facility with machinery, seeming to know by instinct how to coax the best out of every motor, but she sat silent, wondering what he had in mind for her.

Certainly not a straight trip home, or he wouldn't have brought clothes like these, she thought, eyeing the slender lines of her feet in her best high heels.

It wasn't until he swung the Mercedes on to the main road south that an inkling of what he had in mind came to her. Surely he couldn't be taking her back to Auckland, banishing her? Were her bags in the trunk, packed by a jubilant Moira Fieldgate?

A swift glance at his profile met one slanted her way, mocking, cold as the wind from the south. He was waiting for her to ask what his plans were.

Demurely she glanced down at her hands, consciously relaxing her fingers. She would not give him that pleasure.

Ten minutes later she was glad she had restrained herself. Blase turned the car on to a narrow side road which ran swiftly towards the harbour, turned itself

into someone's drive and climbed a hill to reach a house
tucked under the crest, sheltered from the west and
south and open to a glorious view out over Whangarei
Harbour and the ferocious volcanic peaks that rose over
a thousand feet from the sea to form the Heads.

The drive emptied on to an enormous forecourt,
what would have been the stark bareness of concrete
completely banished by exposed pebbles. It looked like
a courtyard, private, sheltered by an enormous garage
and the house and the hill. A dog appeared in the
doorway of a kennel, his chain rattling. He barked
enquiringly once, but after Blase spoke to him, settled
down in the sun to watch them with sleepy eyes, his
head on his paws.

'Where are we?'

Blase lifted a brow. 'I thought you'd never ask. This
place belongs to friends of mine. They've lent it to me
for the day.'

'I—I beg your pardon?'

He smiled, not a nice smile, and drawled, 'Not for
any nefarious purposes, I promise you. Sonia is not at
all permissive, but she quite understood that I'm not
likely to get a minute alone with you at Blackrocks. So
when I said I had something rather important to discuss with you she suggested that I bring you here.'

'What—important something?'

For answer he leaned over and unclipped her seat-
belt. 'Come inside and I'll tell you.'

Every warning light in her brain had gone on, red
for danger, but she allowed him to help her out of the
car and walked beside him into the lovely house.

'Sit down,' he said from the door of what would
once have been called the drawing room and was now
probably a living room. 'You look as though you could
do with some coffee.'

Something stronger would have been better; Merrin
felt so threatened that she couldn't rest, and after a
moment spent staring at a grey leather armchair as
though it was a Martian she moved across to the enor-

mous sliding glass door, pushed it open and walked out on to the terrace.

It ran the full length of the house, facing just east of north, and below were green hills and paddocks, a stretch of mangroves and then the waters of the harbour, gleaming like a milky opal beneath the sun. Across it was the suburb of Onerahi where the airpost was, and as a backdrop those incredible bushclad peaks Mount Manaia, Bream Head which the Maoris called Tamerangi and Mount Lion, looking like the battle-scarred turrets of some ancient, gigantic stronghold. Offshore Hen Island lay trailing the Chickens, and to the south the shoreline swept in an enormous dune-backed bay to Bream Tail.

To the north, out of sight, lay other smaller harbours, Pataua, Ngunguru and Tutukaka, and beyond them again Blackrocks with its tiny estuary.

Merrin stood for a long moment watching the lazy sweep of a hawk above the green pleasant paddocks, aware for the first time just how strong were the ties binding her to the north. It had soaked into her soul, become as much a part of her as her love for Blase. What she had always believed to be an intense physical attraction between them was for her at least, the kind of love which lasts for ever.

As did the loneliness, the bitter estrangement of the soul which was making her shiver now, too shocked to be able to control her anguish.

'Merrin!' Blase's voice was harsh and she turned swiftly, afraid that if he came out he might see her despair.

'I'm here, taking in the view.' She called on her self-control, elaborating as she walked back through the door, 'It's superb, isn't it? Your friends built in exactly the right place.'

His glance was sharp. 'Yes. I'll bring you to see them one night—the view is equally spectacular then, especially when there's no moon. Sit down. Sonia left coffee, so you don't have to put up with instant.'

'I drink instant most of the time at home,' she said, from the depths of the grey armchair.

He looked at her mockingly, smiling yet watchful. 'Never mind, I won't tell anyone. How's your head?'

'Perfectly all right. How's yours?'

'No problems, thanks to your quick thinking.' A gleam lit the depths of his eyes. 'It was a pity you had to ruin that beautiful dress, though. And your attempts at hair cutting could have been a little more sophisticated.'

Someone had effected rapid repairs to that. The thick fair hair was neatly trimmed, hiding the jagged cut. Merrin's heart moved in her breast as she thought of how much damage could have been done.

'Yes, well, I wasn't working under ideal conditions,' she said lightly, grateful for the excuse the coffee gave her to direct her attention elsewhere.

She heard the slight, opulent sound as Blase lowered himself into another armchair, black leather and this one, starkly modern, and waited.

After a moment he asked, 'Why did you go out into that storm, Merrin?'

'The obvious reason.' Although her whole body was stiff, rigid with control, she managed a shrug. 'You needed help, and I couldn't expect Coralie to go. She was terrified.'

Perhaps some note in her voice angered him. Very coldly he said, 'I hope I don't need to tell you that her fear of the dark isn't assumed.'

'No, of course you don't. I can recognise a phobia when I see one.' She set the coffee cup down on the side table, adding, 'She did her best. I felt sorry for her.'

'She feels that she let me down by refusing to go. I'm afraid she blames you for that.'

His voice was wry. Merrin looked up and smiled, for it was understandable. Coralie had not yet outgrown her childish attitudes; nothing could be more certain than that she would resent Merrin's efforts on

Blase's behalf, even though they were for his ultimate good.

'Well, tell her from me that no one's blaming her,' she said lightly. 'I'd have done the same for anyone.'

'No doubt. Would you have kissed anyone else as you did me?'

The question had all the effect of a brandished knife. Merrin's lashes dropped to hide her complete disarray, but he knew exactly how she was feeling, because he went on to say, 'Why not admit it, Merrin? It would make things so much easier if you stopped hiding behind that wall.'

She said nothing, refusing to look anywhere but at the dark blue carpet. There was a soft noise movement and then Blase was in front of her, his hands grasping hers as he pulled her to her feet.

'If it will make it any easier,' he said ironically, 'I'll say it first. I want you. And I'm going to have you. Now——,' his fingers slid up the sleeves of her elegant blue suit to her elbows and he pulled her a little closer, '—now, Merrin, say it.'

'That I want you?' She spoke to his tie, flatly, without emphasis, for her heart was dying within her. 'Why do you want to hear me tell you? You know. You've always known.'

She flung her head back, eyes bitter, watching him as he smiled, a twisted sardonic movement which told her just how much he hated this power she had over him.

'Yes. Did you really think you could come back to Blackrocks with impunity, Merrin? You must have known me well enough to realise that I don't forgive or forget very easily.'

'I thought—six years is a long time.' She sighed, angry with the treachery bred deep within her nerves and brain. She could feel each individual fingertip on the fine bones of her shoulders, smell the faint masculine scent of him, see beneath the smooth cloth of his jacket to the tanned skin and the strength and grace that enslaved her.

'Had you forgotten?'

'No,' she said wearily, adding with incredible stupidity, 'but it's different for a man.'

'Oh, come now, surely you aren't taking refuge in that old bromide? Do you honestly believe that a woman always loves the first man she sleeps with, that a man goes from affair to affair without feeling anything for his lovers? It's almost as naïve as believing in true love.' The sarcasm in his voice stung, as it was meant to, viciously whipping her emotions.

Turning her head away she said heavily, 'What do you want, Blase?'

'You.'

Pale as death she trembled, then bit her lip, forcing herself to calmness. 'No.'

'Ah, but it's not as easy as that, is it, you beautiful little wanton.' His hands moved, touched her throat, the slender curve of her breast beneath the warmth of her jacket, then dropped to his side. He was smiling. 'Come here.'

'No.'

He said nothing, but she could feel him willing her towards him, and knew with incredible clarity that if she went to him now she was doomed.

'No,' she reiterated huskily, her bent head exposing the nape of her neck. 'I won't become your mistress, Blase.'

'I want you.'

The three words, spoken with such stark hunger, lay between them like the bars of a prison, separating them. Merrin looked down at her hands, clasped them together because they were trembling with the need to go to him. He stood a pace away, his entire concentration bent on her, using his will to compel her to betray herself. She could feel him, suffered the intensity of his resolve with a shrinking fear which made her step away, repeating thickly,

'I will *not* be your mistress, Blase.'

'You want me,' he said silkily. 'You're shaking with the effort to stay still. I'd only have to touch you and you'd be begging me to take you.'

'But you won't, will you?' Her voice firmed as she fought for control, calling on the reserves of strength she had built up over the long years, her determination never again to put her well-being in another's hands. A glance flicked over those hands, long-fingered and lean, cruelly strong, the hands of the man she loved, who both hated and wanted her but felt nothing like the emotion she felt towards him.

He needed her to surrender her hard-won freedom. It seemed that the affront to his pride could only be assuaged if she crawled back to him, forced against her will into the dark power of his sensuality. And once there . . . what? For how long would the bonds which fettered them last? Inevitably the final humiliation would be his rejection of her when the passion she roused in him had been slaked.

'No, I won't touch you,' he said, slowly. 'But you'll come to me, sooner or later. You're desperate for me, you haven't even attempted to deny it. I've waited six years for you—I can wait another few days.'

Pride lifted her head. Crisply, with an emphasis he could not miss, she retorted, 'You'll be waiting for longer than that! You forget, I know what happens to your mistresses! Only an idiot would court disaster a second time.'

'Nevertheless, you'll do it,' he promised, smiling with lazy mockery, his expression keen as a bird of prey sighting a victim. 'How many other men have you had, besides your husband and me?'

Colour washed over her pale face in a great tide. With a swift sideways glance at him she moved back to the chair, sinking into it with gratitude, turning to take up her coffee. 'That's none of your business,' she said, watching as her breath made little gold-brown cats-paws across the liquid. 'I don't ask you questions like that.'

'Feel free.'

She looked up, met the cold cynicism of his glance and bit her lip. 'Oh, for heaven's sake, Blase,' she began dully. 'I'm not interested. I don't care. Will you stop nagging at me! I want to go home.'

The cup trembled on its saucer; very carefully she put it on the occasional table, fighting for the control not to burst into tears.

Blase stood still for a moment, his glance burning into her. Then he said quite gently, 'Very well, then, let's go home.'

CHAPTER NINE

LATER that evening, after Merrin had been sent to bed by Hope, Ellis came in to see her, carefully leaving the door open as he came through it.

'In case anyone gets the wrong idea,' he told her, looking mischievous. 'How are you, my dear? And I mean it, so don't just airily say you're fine, like you've told everyone else.'

'Well, if it's truth you want, I've got a headache, and I feel ever so slightly rocky on my pins.' Merrin put aside her copy of *Dragonflight* with a smile. It was easy enough to confess to these slight disabilities; she wasn't going to tell him that it was the session with Blase which had caused them.

'Could be worse, I suppose. Blase says you're to rest, at least all of tomorrow.' His glance invited her reaction to this piece of arbitrariness.

Merrin smiled, wishing it could be more spontaneous. 'He suffers from an over-developed sense of responsibility. A good night's sleep is all I need. Have you incorporated the cloudburst into the book?'

Chuckling, he said, 'Yes, with great effect. Not that I've done much of it. We've been busy around the place, repairing fences, and roads, moving stock.'

'You?'

'Me. I know you consider me absolutely useless, but I can do a few things, you know.' He grinned and patted her hand, to show he didn't mean it. 'Blase has been working like a demon, co-ordinating help for the whole area. He should have been resting, but the man is made of iron. Still, the worst seems to be over now.' He paused, then went on quietly, 'You did well, Merrin, but I don't have to tell you that, I know. I'm very proud of you.'

'Why—thank you!' Touched, she smiled at him. 'But it's Blase you should be admiring! He took the full force of that wretched boulder, and he hasn't had a night in hospital to recover.'

'He didn't walk through the rain for an hour or so, either,' Ellis said quietly. 'Now, I'd better go. Oh, by the way, did you know that the pretty little Coralie threw the father and mother of a tantrum here yesterday morning?' Ellis was a gossip, without malice but with an intense interest in what made his fellow humans tick.

Merrin moved uneasily against her pillows, the elaborate brass bedside lamp swinging gently on its chains in the breeze from the window. 'No. She's very young, of course.'

'Old enough to know better, the little brat. She wanted Blase to take her home, back to the Allens' place, and when he told her, quite politely, that he had more pressing things to do she blew her top.' Another pause, and a very sharp glance. 'Your name was mentioned several times.'

'Oh, *hell*!' Merrin pressed a hand to her throbbing temples.

'Would you like to tell me about it? I do feel a certain responsibility for whatever situation you've found yourself in, and don't try to tell me there isn't one. I've studiously avoided poking around, but the tension between you and Blase makes the atmosphere crackle and spit sparks. Our gracious hostess is on edge, the housekeeper would like nothing better than to see you gone, and you, my dear, have lost weight and are beginning to look haunted. All my doing. If I hadn't insisted on you coming with me none of this would have happened.'

'Do you think so?' Merrin sighed, touched by his evident concern. 'I'm beginning to feel it was inevitable.'

'Perhaps.' He took her hands in a warm clasp, his thin, ironic face serious as he surveyed her slight figure against the bank of pillows. 'With all the inevitability of a Greek tragedy. I should have realised, knowing Blase. I did realise it. He's never been the sort to forgive easily. Once you lost his trust that was it.'

His touch was wonderfully comforting, but she could not allow him to go on blaming himself. 'Rubbish,' she said as briskly as she could, smiling warmly. 'It's not your fault I'm permanently fixated on a man who loathes me.'

'No, but it's my fault we're here. I must confess that I was interested in the situation, curious to see what would happen. That's why I pressed so hard for you to come.' Ellis looked at their clasped hands, smiled with wry self-knowledge and said softly, 'A mischief-maker, I'm afraid, and I've been punished for my presumption, but not as much as you, my dear. Or Blase, I'm afraid. He's not happy. Would you like to go home?'

'Yes, please,' she sighed.

'Very well, then.' He squeezed her fingers, then released them, smiling with the lopsided grin that revealed how well he knew his own failings. 'Too late and too little, I'm afraid, but I can only say I'm sorry and promise not to treat people as puppets any more.'

'You're a darling,' she said impulsively, and bent over and kissed his cheek, adding, 'Wicked, I'll admit, but a darling nevertheless.'

'And you're far too forgiving. Goodnight.'

He walked across to the door, stopped as he reached it and said over his shoulder, 'Couldn't you summon up some of that mercy for Blase, Merrin? I think he needs it more than I do.'

Merrin stared, taken aback at his remark. It seemed completely irrelevant. It was she who needed compassion, not Blase. He was hunting her down, using her weaknesses with skill to drive her into a relationship which could only lead to disaster. For them both, she thought wearily, recalling the desperate craving in his face and voice as he told her that he wanted her. He hated himself for his weakness, but he could no more resist it than she could.

What kind of hunger was this, this unbearable starving need? Strong enough to bind them together after six years, consummated not just once but scores of times over a year, and yet still it was not satisfied. Blase had used one of the decadent poets of the nineteenth century to categorise it, calling it an old passion, one that he was desolate and sick of. Merrin turned her head into the pillow, remembering the lines:

> I cried for madder music and stronger wine,
> But when the feast is finished and the lamps expire,
> Then falls thy shadow, Cynara!

Dowson might have been a minor poet, but he knew what he was talking about, she thought cynically, filled with self-contempt. Perhaps Blase was right. Perhaps they should become lovers once more in the hope of ridding themselves of this degrading passion, for degrading it was. No greater shame could be imagined than to love a man who not only despised her but despised himself for wanting her.

Pain splintered behind her eyes. With a muffled whimper she turned her head into the pillow, unable to ease herself in tears.

Hope's voice was almost gentle. 'I did knock, but ...' She looked down at Merrin's pale averted face, and for a moment the bland, self-righteous mask slipped. Merrin saw the woman behind it and closed her eyes. Not that, too, not Hope's pains and terrors and guilts; she could not bear it.

'The doctor left some tablets for you,' the older woman told her quietly. 'I'll get them for you, and some water.'

She was gone only a few moments, moments Merrin used to compose her face. She was exhausted, her lips pale, long lashes casting a shadow across the satin of her cheeks.

Hope, too, seemed to have regained her composure.

She watched while Merrin took the tablets, then said, 'I've just been talking to Ellis. He tells me you're going soon.'

Wearily, Merrin nodded. A faintly queasy feeling kept her attention focused on the silk draperies at the window.

'He'll tell Blase tonight, I suppose.' Hope's voice was oddly uncertain. Hope, who had never been unsure of anything in her life!

Merrin said tonelessly, 'Yes, I suppose so.'

'Merrin, I want you to know that—that I've never—I've not had anything personally against you. Ever. I didn't know that you and Blase knew each other so well when I—when I . . .' She stopped, and turned away, unable to say exactly what she had done. 'I love Blase, more than I loved Terry. I wouldn't have hurt him. When I realised what a great wrong I'd done him I told him. He found Terry, but by then you'd married. I was glad, I hoped you were happy. After Blase had rid Blackrocks of every sign of your presence here I hoped that he, too, would be able to forget. Calf love burns itself out.'

Merrin lifted her lashes, weary and cold. She did not want to hear Hope's stumbling explanation of her motives; she could feel the older woman's anguish and embarrassment, her anger. Hope hated being forced to face her tangle of treachery.

'It doesn't matter,' she said drearily. 'It's all over.'

'No, it's not. Do you think I'd be telling you this if I didn't feel I had to? Blase has made it quite clear that he doesn't intend to marry Coralie, and that can only be because you've come back.'

'Were you so sure of it before?'

Hope gestured, her anger barely held in check, the fine features tight. 'As sure of it as anyone can be with Blase,' she said bitterly. 'He doesn't show his feelings, but he liked her and, everyone knows, she's pretty enough.' She took a deep breath, fought for control and attained it, managing to resume in her usual even tones, 'I don't know what it is about you that attracts men—as a woman, I suppose I'm at a disadvantage. But whatever it is, Blase can't resist it. I'm not stupid—I've been watching you together and it's obvious. I came to tell you that when he marries I intend to buy a house in Whangarei. You needn't worry about having me here.'

'And Moira?' asked poor Merrin, by now so tense that she could feel prickles of stress along her skin and nerves.

'Moira? What has Moira Fieldgate to do with anything?'

'Just that she's warned me off too.'

Hope stared at her, her brows elevating in disbelief. 'Then she has had no right to, at all! Moira is a treasure, as I'm sure you're well aware, but that doesn't give her the right to meddle in our affairs.'

Spoken with true Stanhope arrogance, Merrin decided. Aloud she said, 'Possibly I misunderstood her.'

'I hope so.' By now Hope was fully in command of herself. 'I must go—your eyes are starting to droop. I hope that what I've told you will clear the air between us. Goodnight, Merrin.'

'Goodnight.'

Merrin watched her out of sight, her eyes lingering on the closed door, her tired brain trying in vain to assimilate just what Hope had told her. Only one thing was clear. That Blase knew the truth, and he had not told her, had acted as though he still believed that she had been Terry's lover and ally. Why?

When she woke in the morning, of course, her subconscious had been busy and the answer was clear. The betrayal which had hurt was her marriage to Paul, and probably, her pregnancy. He said that he knew everything about her marriage, but he could not know how advanced her pregnancy was, so he could not know that the child was his.

And he could not know of the tensions in that ill-fated marriage which had finally torn it apart. No, in his eyes she had left without trying to clear her name and proved her perfidy by immediately marrying another man.

So he had immediately begun escorting the exorbitantly beautiful Australian model who had wanted to marry him. There must have been others between her and Coralie, for he was a virile man. Merrin winced, remembering the joy they had had in each other, her delight in discovering what pleased him, his tenderness and sweet violence. They seemed to have been made for each other in those long nights when his passion had made her physically a woman. Not emotionally or mentally, though, she thought drearily, or that marriage with Paul would never have happened. It was a child who had left Blackrocks and allowed Paul to persuade her against her better instincts; maturity had come with her appreciation of what she had done to him.

Perhaps it was always so. No wonder so many teenage marriages failed! Had Blase ever got around to marrying her perhaps the end would have been the same—bitterness and despair, the underlying cynicism that motivated him proving too strong for the love they bore each other.

Calf love, perhaps, but so strong that they were still enmeshed in it, unable to break free from its dark enchantment.

Sighing, Merrin turned her head from the pillows to look across at the windows. Outside it was dreary, low clouds and a thin wind tossing the sunburst heads of the papyrus reed against the white wall. Whatever drug Hope had given her had left her thick and fuzzy in the head. From the dampness of her pillow she deduced that she had spent some of the night crying. She could not remember her dreams, but the after-effect still lingered, leaving her feeling extraordinarily fragile.

Pushing the dark clouds of depression away, she climbed out of bed, showered and washed her hair, touching with careful fingers the graze on her scalp. Thank heavens for young blood, she thought, feeling about eighty. It was healing remarkably quickly, but she towelled it gingerly, then sat on her bed, using the drier, her head bent as she fought her mood and the weather.

Moira's arrival with a tray startled her.

'Oh—you shouldn't have bothered!' she exclaimed. 'I know how busy you are in the mornings.'

'It's no bother.' Nothing to be gained from that impassive face. 'Hop back into bed and I'll put it across you knees. It's too cold to be sitting around.'

Merrin sighed, but settled herself back against the pillows. 'I'm not an invalid,' she said mutinously. 'I'll bet Blase isn't having breakfast in bed! He was more badly hurt than I was.'

The housekeeper smiled frostily as she straightened a spoon. 'He has a harder head. No headaches for him! And this is on his orders, so eat it up.'

It certainly looked delectable—fruit juice and a half grapefruit, with toast and coffee in a small china pot. And in a little pottery container a cluster of the last of the roses, deep crimson with a faint, elusive perfume.

'Thank you.' Merrin smiled, adding firmly, 'But I am *not* spending the rest of the day in bed.'

'Well, that depends on Blase.'

'Oh no, it doesn't,' said Merrin, but she said it beneath her breath to Moira's back as the housekeeper moved out of the room. While she ate the grapefruit Merrin found herself wondering why Moira felt it so necessary to keep aloof from those around her. Perhaps it was her character; she certainly knew her place and she made sure that no one else encroached on it. Had Moira been a little more approachable the younger Merrin would not have been so unprotected six years ago.

Even as the thought came to her Merrin dismissed it. Mora could have been the most motherly soul in the world, but she would have been unable to shelter her from Blase's desire. And Merrin had not wanted any protection. She had gone with the thoughtless confidence of youth into his arms, so secure in her own reading of the situation that the idea of resisting him had never occurred to her.

Well, she was making up for it how, she thought grimly, leaning back against the pillows. But the sooner she got away from Blackrocks the better. She had no illusions about her strength of will compared to Blase's, and if he persisted in trying to seduce her again sooner or later he would succeed. As he had almost succeeded several times since she had come back. It was only the fact that he wanted to break her, to force her to come to him, that had kept her from his bed.

Restlessly she pushed back the covers, shivering slightly. The rooms were heated, but Blase was an ardent conservationist and the central heating was set so low that it only took the chill off the air. Winter had truly arrived, cold and bleak today, but here in the North tomorrow could be another exquisite day of gold and blue, with the sea sparkling with laughter against the smiling land.

Meanwhile Merrin pulled on slacks and a thin polo-necked jersey beneath a matching jacket, combed her hair once more and applied enough make-up to hide her pallor. Quietly she moved along the hallway, past the kitchen, redolent of newly-baked bread and something else which was probably the scent of an enormous pot of pea and ham soup.

All was quiet. An hour or so ago she had heard the Range Rover take off, so that removed Blase from the scene; probably Ellis had gone with him. As the kitchen was empty Moira must be working around the house. Merrin washed and dried her dishes and left them neatly arrayed on the bench before heading off to her office.

Once there it was impossible not to catch up on her work. If it did nothing else, she thought half-grimly, it would keep her too busy to worry about herself or the unhappiness which clouded her whole being.

As usual she became thoroughly engrossed in her work to the point of not hearing the sound as the connecting door between her room and Blase's office opened.

She was soon made aware of it, however. A lean finger stabbed the dictaphone to silence; Blase bent down and jerked her from her seat, his lips compressed in a way that told her he was extremely angry.

'Didn't I leave instructions for you to stay in bed?' he demanded, shaking her.

'Yes.' She wriggled, but he refused to release her. 'I'm not an invalid. Blase, leave me alone.'

'I can't,' he ground out before he kissed her, forcing her head back so far that the skin across her throat was stretched to pain. His mouth plundered hers, hurting her, then softening into a demand so piercingly sweet that she closed her eyes and swayed against him, his hands in the smooth dark honey of his hair.

'Please help me, I can't,' he said thickly, his heart driving into hers with a familiar urgency. 'When are you going to give in, Merrin?' He was pale beneath his year-round tan, the hazel of his eyes lit by fires behind them to an almost pure gold.

Slowly she lowered her hands, holding them clasped against his chest, feeling the pace of his heart beat steady and then begin to ease. 'I'm not,' she said in numb anguish. 'Give me credit for some sense of self-preservation. You nearly destroyed me once—I won't let it happen again.'

'You won't be able to prevent it.' His voice was heavy and raw, compelling in its purposefulness.

As Merrin shook her head he released her, thrusting his hands into his pockets as if they had betrayed him while the flames in his eyes died down. A sardonic smile touched his mouth, for she stepped away so swiftly that she tripped and only saved herself from falling by grabbing at his arm.

'You're hooked, and you know it,' he told her softly. 'Like a bird caught in a net—the harder you struggle the more entangled you become. There's no way out, Merrin.'

She tossed her head, angry with him for his cynical appraisal of the situation, even angrier with herself because he was right and she knew it as well as he did. One of the pages of the manuscript fluttered to the floor; she welcomed the chance to bend and pick it up, freed for a moment from the derisive speculation in his gaze.

'What about Coralie?' The question came unbidden to her lips, startling her.

'What about her?'

Colour touched her cheeks. She stacked the pages of typescript, put them into a folder and opened a drawer to slide them in. 'I thought you had her in mind for a wife.'

'Indeed?' He sounded amused, almost indulgent. 'No. She's a child. She'll end up marrying Dave Appleton some day. He worships the ground she walks on!'

'Does she realise that you were just flirting with her?'

His hand curved around the back of her neck, the strong fingers moving sensuously over her skin. 'Jealous, Merrin?' he whispered.

She stared at him, then abruptly lowered her lashes and tried to pull away. Instantly Blase's fingers clenched on the roots of her hair.

'Answer me,' he said. 'Are you jealous of Coralie?' 'No.'

From beneath her lashes she could see the way his mouth quirked. A pulse beat beside the clean sculptured lines of it, revealing that he was as affected by her closeness as she was by his. Her breath came rapidly through her lips. She had to fight an overwhelming urge to give in to his merciless pursuit, allow herself to be submerged by his desire for her. Only the memories of what it was like when his passion was displaced by anger gave her the strength to resist.

He lowered his head, brushing the sensitive hollow

below her ear with his lips as he spoke. 'I've always treated Coralie as a charming younger sister. If she chose to make pretty little schemes that's her fault, not mine.'

'You're heartless,' she accused crisply, remembering the hunger in Coralie's eyes when they had rested on him.

'Ever heard of the old saw that sometimes it's necessary to be cruel to be kind? I'm beginning to think it should be a maxim to live by.' His mouth teased the lobe of her ear, the tip of his tongue gently tracing the intricate spiral there. 'You've satisfied your pride,' he whispered. 'You've kept me dangling, made me well aware that you despise me and yourself, but you know that however much you struggle there's no way out. Whatever there is between us affects both of us, and the only way we we're going to be able to free ourselves from it is to let it take its course.'

'I will *not* be your live-in mistress!' she snapped, her voice hard with determination. She pushed away from him and turned, eyes very bright as they took in the beloved contours of his face, disturbing, dangerous as he smiled.

'You will.' He spoke with such complete conviction that she shivered, but defiance lit her eyes to emeralds. He grinned suddenly, leaned forward and pinched her chin, momentarily the old Blase who had been big brother to her during the day and lover at night. 'And if you're good I might even give you a present.'

Swinging on his heel, he left, whistling between his teeth as though something pleased him. Merrin stared after him, one hand on the place his fingers had touched while tears gathered beneath her lashes.

Fortune smiled on her. He was out for dinner—something to do with the flood, Ellis told her absently. After dinner Merrin watched television for an hour or so with a very silent Hope, then made her way to her room, sick at heart and weary as she had never been before.

Instinct warned her that their affairs were building up to a climax. Hope apparently thought that Blase intended to marry her; as she took her clothes off prior to having a bath Merrin smiled ironically. Poor Hope had never really emerged from life in the forties when nice girls were virgins until their wedding night and it was only men who were allowed to sow wild oats. Just what she would say if she knew exactly what her beloved nephew planned for Merrin was hard to imagine. Shock, horrified incredulity—she would run the whole gamut of emotions and still end up thinking that the situation must somehow be Merrin's fault.

As it was, in one way. If stupidity was the greatest sin, then she was certainly being punished for it.

But she could hold him off until they left she would be safe—surely she had that much willpower. He would not rape her. Even if he did, she thought, her fingers shaking as she undid her bra, he could not force her to stay here. Not even to herself would she admit that the deep wrenching ache in her loins was not revulsion at the thought of being raped.

She ran her bath, flung in an expensive bath oil perfumed with tuberose and got in, determined to soak away her despair. On the vanity bench her transistor told her what tunes had sold the most in New Zealand that week, a mixture of hard rock and syrupy pop. Deliberately she forced herself to relax, reading one of her old favourites, *Cold Comfort Farm*.

It was an hour later that she finally climbed out. She felt almost relaxed enough to go to sleep. Only physically, of course. For once *Cold Comfort Farm* had failed its usual magic and her thoughts were still whirling around in her brain, futile, enervating thoughts which couldn't hide the fact that she was as much in love with Blase as she had been when she was an innocent sixteen-year-old.

Wearily she dried herself, stretching her taut slim body. The scent of the tuberoses in the bath oil still lingered, heavy on the warm damp air. What on earth did Blase possess that so fascinated her that she was unable to break free of him? In the years since she had left Blackrocks she had met plenty of other men, many just as good-looking, some with that superb physical presence which made a handsome face unnecessary, even a few with his kind of inborn command and authority. He was clever and sophisticated, but she had met men who were brilliant and felt not the slightest attraction to them or any others. Somehow, somewhere, they dovetailed, the sensual magic they created together strong enough to make everything else seem unimportant.

But she had learnt her lesson and learnt it well. Without respect and tenderness and liking there could be only that physical hunger and by itself it was fairy's gold, turning to dead leaves in the hand. She would not put her life in jeopardy again because Blase brought every nerve in her body to singing life.

Sighing, she switched off the transistor and pulled her dressing gown on, hauling up the zip which fastened it with a vicious movement of her hand. She opened the door and walked into the bedroom and Blase saluted her with the glass of wine he was drinking and stood up from the edge of the bed and smiled at her, his eyes roving with insolent freedom down the body beneath the velvet of her gown.

'Get the hell out of here!' Merrin was so angry that the words snapped out between her lips one at a time, like bullets.

He laughed, and drained the wine, setting the glass down on the bedside table. 'Sorry,' he said, quite gently, 'but we have a few things to settle between us.'

Merrin tried not to be obvious as she measured the distance to the door. 'Everything is settled,' she retorted. 'You'll just have to mark me up as the one that got away.'

'It's locked.' He grinned at her sudden exclamation. 'What a nasty word! You'd better have some wine to take the taste of it away.'

Very steadily Merrin said, 'I don't want any wine,
Blase. I don't want anything but a good night's sleep.
Will you please go!'

'No.' He came towards her, watching with a kind of
amused understanding as she backed away. 'You're
shaking,' he taunted when the wall prevented her from
going any further. 'Are you afraid of me, my darling?'

Very slowly his hand reached out and he traced the
line of her mouth with a fingertip before wrenching
the zip down to reveal that she was naked beneath the
velvet.

'You're beautiful,' he said between his teeth as he
prevented her hands from dragging the opening together. 'And you're mine. You always have been. By
the time I've finished with you, my lady, you'll have
forgotten that you ever let another man touch you like
this . . .' His hand probed beneath the gown, closed on
her breast. 'I could kill you . . .' he breathed.

'Other men,' she said harshly.

The long fingers tightened hurtfully, then relaxed.
He moved closer, looking down at her with hard
amusement. 'No, Merrin, I know there've been no
others. Ellis told me one night, after his second brandy,
that until you confessed your scarlet past he'd thought
you frigid. No men.'

'Damn you!'

'Probably,' he agreed, and lifted the hand which held
hers still, kissing the fingers in a parody of Continental
amorousness. Above the slender pallor of her hands he
surveyed her infuriated face, his eyes aglint with
mockery and the leafing lights of passion. Against her
breast his hand was gentle but inexorable, fondling the
soft weight, the gentle curves. 'Beautiful,' he said
again.

Merrin's eyes blazed with outrage and fury. 'Let me
alone!' she hissed, suddenly twisting beneath his
hands.

Instantly they tightened, and then he moved, sweeping the gown from her shoulders to the floor, his ex-

pression stripped of everything but a rage of hunger
which terrified Merrin.

'You're in my blood.' His voice was rough and
uneven as he swept her into his arms and took her
across to the bed. 'In my brain, in my guts, part of
me . . .'

She struggled, pushing at him, her face contorted
with fear and anger and pain, for he was not gentle
with her. Drawing a sobbing breath, she raked her fin-
gernails across his shoulders, biting him, writhing until
he held her still by rolling on to her and using his
weight to press her into the yielding mattress so that
she could not bring her knees up to his groin.

Blase smiled as his head came down to hers. He had
her wrists, one in each hand and he pushed them beneath her buttocks until he could hold them both together in one of his. He used the same hand to haul
her closer so that she was half suffocated beneath his
weight, but he did not kiss her, merely watched with
the hot gold of his gaze engulfing her as she fought
him frantically.

'Merrin . . .' he said at last, when she lay still and
exhausted in his grip, watching the tormented rise and
fall of her breast. And his head came the last few inches
and his mouth touched her averted cheek, gentle,
moving slowly across the fing skin.

She shivered. The hairs at the back of her neck lifted
as his tongue traced a path to beneath her ear. She had
expected an onslaught, but he was showing her how
sweet his desire could be.

She turned her head, pleading with him to stop, her
green eyes terrified. 'I don't want you, Blase,' she
whispered. 'Please, don't.'

'You don't know what you want.' His free hand came
up and touched her breast, the strong fingers possessive as they touched and stroked until her terror and
anger began to fade, to be replaced by exquisite sensations, at once familiar and forgotten.

His mouth drifted lower, touching the most sensitive

parts of her throat and shoulders, settled at last on her breast. Between kisses he wooed her with his voice, telling her that she was beautiful . . . beautiful . . . that he had waited so long for her . . .

Merrin lay still, staring at the ceiling, her mind screaming in outrage, her body playing the traitor, for his voice and his mouth and his hands were appealing to the most primitive and the most powerful court there is, and she knew that against the hunger deep within her she had no further defences. And Blase knew so well how to arouse that hunger; even now his hand was fondling the curve of her hip, the faint swell of her stomach, smoothing the long line of her thighs. Deep within her loins a fire began to burn. She caught her breath and he looked up and kissed her mouth, teasing her lips apart, gentle until she relaxed in submission beneath him.

She could have ensured it better had he been rough with her but except that he refused to free her he was tormentingly tender, worshipping her body with every skill, every ounce of knowledge at his command, teasing, frustrating, until she was bereft of any other desire but that of slaking her hunger in his strength.

'Darling,' he muttered, releasing her hands so that he could cup her face.

Wild-eyed, she stared at him. He was holding on a tight rein, his jaw and mouth almost grim as he fought and controlled his basic instinct to take her. Her lashes flickered. With a heart-deep sigh Merrin lifted her hands and pulled his shirt open fiercely, glad that she ripped two buttons off. He smiled, shrugged free from it and kissed her again, his mouth suddenly grown cruel. Her hands moved across his shoulders, slowly over the bunched muscles beneath that smooth skin, descended to his waist and felt for the buckle of his pants.

She reacted to the shudder that engulfed him with a slow savage smile. 'Darling,' she whispered, taunting him, lowering her lashes so that her expression was hidden.

'Undress me.'

She took her time about it. Desire made her wanton; she kissed and fondled him as he had touched her until at last he made a muffled sound deep in his throat and she saw the tough mask of his features crack as his passions began to ride him and he lost control.

Then there was nothing but sensation, a sunburst of sensation which engulfed her so that she moaned her excitement against his shoulder, only barely conscious of the dampness of his skin. She remembered exactly how to move, gloried in the strength of him, even smiled as tension began to spiral upwards into ecstasy.

'Now deny it,' Blase said thickly, a long time after.

Tears shimmered beneath her closed lids, over-flowed, and he said in a wrenched voice, 'Oh, *God*! Merrin, my little love, my sweet delight, don't cry. All these years—all the bitter long years—I've wanted you so, and since you've come back to me all I've done is hurt you. Please don't cry. Now now.'

'I c-can't help it . . .' But she could, for when the meaning of his words hit her the tears dried and she lay very still. His arms were hard and strong around her, but his hand as it touched her cheek was wonder-fully gentle and tender. She shivered as he wiped away the tears, following his finger with his lips, soft against the smooth satin of her skin.

'I love you,' she said harshly, keeping her eyes tight shut.

'I know.' He sighed and touched his mouth to hers. 'I love you too. Always.'

Merrin's lashes flew up in total bewilderment. He smiled and whispered against her mouth, 'Didn't you guess, darling fool? I knew on my twenty-first birth-day. Remember? You came up after school and ran me to earth in the study and gave me a book on wading birds.'

She nodded. 'I remember.' Oh, how clearly she remembered. She had been wide-eyed at the preparations for the party that evening, envious because she was too young to go. For weeks she had saved her pocket money to buy Blase the book and she was still panicked by the thought that she had chosen wrongly. So she had dressed in her best summer frock and wrapped her gift as beautifully as she could in navy blue paper with red stripes, tied a scarlet ribbon bow to it and carried it up.

Blase had been busy in the study, but he greeted her with that swift glinting smile which always roused such bewildering sensations within her. Her voice left her; she had whispered 'Happy Birthday,' and poked the parcel at him. And he had put his arm around her shoulders and held her loosely for a moment before opening it. Relief mingled with the excitement when she saw him smile. She knew that he liked it. And he had said, 'Don't I get a birthday kiss, Merrin?'

Colour stained her cheeks and she looked up at him. He had been in a teasing mood, but the laughter had died from his eyes as she stood on tiptoe and gravely pressed her lips against his. He had tensed and then his arms were across her back and he kissed her briefly, very gently, before letting her go. It had been her first kiss.

'Yes, I remember,' she said again, huskily. 'You—you were very gentle.'

'When you kissed me with your serious little face I knew that I had to have you.' He smiled wryly at her astonishment and turned his mouth into the soft warmth of her throat. 'You were so sweet and you used to look at me with those great eyes, devouring me, totally unconscious of what you were doing to me. I was going to wait until you were twenty, then marry you. But then your mother died and your father headed out to sea. At first I was pleased; I had you in the house and I could make sure that no one else got to you. I should have packed you off to boarding school; you were too much of a temptation. What happened was inevitable. I thought I could control myself, but the first time you melted against me I was lost. I wanted you so much, and the young are greedy.'

He feathered a row of kisses up to the lobe of her ear, soft, tantalising movements that made her skin prickle. Merrin sighed, unable to speak, unable to move.

'I didn't care who knew,' he admitted. 'But for your sake I made sure that we kept our affair quiet. I didn't want anyone lifting an eyebrow at you. And then I realised that I was being totally unfair to you.'

'Unfair?' Astonished, she turned, eyes wide open as they took in the hard incisive line of his profile.

'Yes.' He kissed her, softly, gently, but when she moaned and clung he put her away and got up, totally unashamed of his nudity, and walked across to the table. He poured wine into the glasses and brought them back.

He was a superb animal, Merrin thought dreamily, watching the play of muscles beneath the smooth skin, her eyes at last free to roam the wide shoulders and spare waist, the lean flat stomach and strong, heavily-muscled thighs.

'If you stare at me like that we'll never finish what we have to say,' Blase teased as he gave her the wine. 'You have the most smouldering eyes of anyone I've ever seen. When we made love you used to close your eyes when I kissed you, cool as a naiad, and then you would lift your lashes and your eyes would be raven-ous, deep enough to drown in.' He drank, watching as colour flooded her skin. 'I was obsessed with you,' he said roughly. 'I still am. I would have died for you. And I knew that although you thought you loved me you felt nothing so potent for me. With you it was almost entirely physical. Anything else was hero-wor-ship.'

'No, that's not true.' She was trying to be objective, but her voice trembled. It was suddenly very important to convince him of this. 'I did love you, as much as I was able to. I was childish, I know, but I—you were my whole world. That was why I couldn't bear it when you took Terry's word against mine.'

That coldly formidable toughness came back into his expression, hardening his features. 'Yes,' he said sombrely, 'but if I'd been more confident of your love I'd never have believed him. The fault was mine, entirely; I suppose my conscience harassed me. I couldn't rid myself of the guilt I felt every time I kissed you. I'd seduced you before you were old enough to know what you were doing, and the fact that you fell into my hand like a ripe plum only intensified my fear that your love was almost purely physical.'

She nodded, understanding. 'Hope told me that she told you the truth about that evening. When, Blase?'

'About ten days after you'd gone. I know you don't have much time for Hope and heaven knows, she deserves your censure. But she has her own code. I don't honestly think she knew that I—that we were lovers. When she realised that I was almost out of my mind she admitted that you'd been with her. By that time Terry had disappeared. It took me a while to find him. When I did I beat the truth out of him.'

She gasped, horrified by the bleak savagery in his voice. 'Blase—you didn't!'

'Oh yes, and I'd be lying if I said it didn't give me great pleasure.' He spoke with such chilling ferocity that she shrank back against the pillows, aware once more of his great capacity for violence and the immense self-command he had cultivated to keep it under control.

'Dear Blase!' Shivering, she drank some of the wine, feeling it slide down her throat with a pleasure that showed her how badly off balance she was.

He smiled without amusement, his eyes cold as they swept the taut length of her body against the satin pillows. 'So, then I had to find you. That took a while, and when I did you were married. Not only married, but clearly pregnant.' He set the glass down on the bedside table, came around and took hers from her, his expression shuttered, icy with control. 'So I knew then just how little you had felt for me.' A cynical smile pulled his lips back, almost into a snarl. 'It was just as well I sent a detective after you, because if I'd been the one to catch up with you I'd have killed you, I think.' He reached for her, his expression icily impassive.

'Blase . . .' She was afraid, afraid of the anguish that fuelled his anger, afraid that she had killed that love which had been so fresh and wondrous. 'Oh—Blase!' she whispered, suffering the cruelty of his hands without flinching because his pain was hers. 'I married Paul because I was pregnant. The baby was yours. I was desperate and he—he said he'd look after me.'

For one dreadful moment Blase's body twisted in a spasm of agony. Then he muttered something so thickly that she couldn't hear him before he knelt beside the bed, hands holding his head, and said wearily, 'I should have known. Why didn't I know?'

'It doesn't matter,' she whispered, stroking the thick hair back. 'Darling, it doesn't matter. It's all right.'

He came beside her, holding her in an embrace which was without passion until the trembling had eased. Against the hard smooth surface of his shoulder she said in a voice empty of emotion, 'Paul was only twenty and he tried, but he couldn't—I used to think of you when——' She shivered, remembering. Blase's arms tightened so that she could feel the heavy thunder of his heartbeats against her cheek. 'I killed him, Blase, just as much as if I fired a bullet into him. He hated himself and hated me because I was responsible for his failings.'

'Don't . . .' His voice was agonised. 'Darling, don't, I beg of you.'

'I must. He—he deserves that, at least, that I make you understand.' She fought for control, waiting until the tremors that racked her body ceased before continuing, 'He was so young, and so was I. Too young to know how to cope with his jealousy and too young to be able to hide that whenever he touched me I wanted you. He—he hit me once, and I fell down a flight of stairs and lost the baby. He waited until he knew that I was going to be all right and then he drove the car into the river. If I hadn't married him he would have found himself a wife who loved him and he would be alive today.' She lifted her head, willing him to understand, to cease his hatred of Paul. 'Now do you see?' she whispered. 'I killed him.'

'So you've been dragging round a burden of guilt ever since,' Blase said harshly. 'You didn't kill him, Merrin. He killed himself. But even if you did, do you think he would have wanted you to punish yourself for the rest of your life for his weakness?'

She sighed, remembering Paul with his laughter and his cocky self-assurance, his awkward gentleness. No, Paul would not want her to be guilty. It was his own guilt which had driven him into the river. A life for a life, he had written in the note he left behind, the one she had destroyed.

'No, I suppose not,' she said, 'but I can't forgive myself. I knew when I married him that all the love I was capable of feeling had been given. What happened was my fault.'

'Then you must try.' He kissed her, gently yet with a strength of possession which had her sighing blissfully. 'Don't *do* that . . .' he muttered unsteadily, and then, against the sweet curve of her mouth, 'Oh, how I've *missed* you! I can live without you, but without you my life is very dull music, my heart.'

'I don't believe that.' It was exquisite to be able to tease him softly from the fullness of her heart, to feel the warmth of his limbs around her, holding her, loving her. 'You had Blackrocks. And an assortment of ladies.'

'An assortment?' He rolled over on to his back, staring up at the ceiling with eyes oddly startled. 'There have been one or two other women, but they meant nothing. And you talk of guilt—well, I feel guilty about them.' He turned his head as she lifted herself up on an elbow and gazed down into his face. A wry smile touched the cruel line of his lips.

'Can one be unfaithful to a mistress?' she asked gently, knowing exactly how he felt.

'To me you've always been my wife. That was why I couldn't believe it when you married. It seemed like the worst kind of betrayal. The thought of you in someone else's arms almost drove me mad. Night after night I'd lie in bed imagining you——' he broke off as Merrin winced and bent her head to his chest, wrapping her arms around him as if to protect him.

After a moment he clamped an arm around her shoulders, saying harshly, 'It didn't help at all to know that I'd driven you away with my bloody-minded jealousy. When Hope told me what she'd done I could have killed her. I almost did kill Terry. If I'd known then that you'd married I think I would have. It got so much that I had that stupid affair with Sophie, just to prove to myself that I could find forgetfulness. And for all the good it did I should have stayed at home. No other woman,' he said fiercely, lifting her to lie above him, 'never any other woman. Only you, ever since the first time I saw you, I think. You were a little scrap, neat and soft-spoken, not beautiful but with too much character in your face to be pretty. I was eighteen, and I was glad I only saw you during the holidays from varsity because you stuck in my mind. I thought it was unnatural to be so interested in a child.'

Merrin nodded, resting her mouth on the strong warm column of his neck. 'I know. It was like that for me too.'

'I should have married you the minute you turned sixteen,' he said against her forehead. 'Then none of this would have happened.'

'I was only a child when I left here,' she murmured. 'Too immature for marriage.'

'How about now? It takes about three days to get a licence. Will you marry me then?'

She smiled, although her eyes were misted with tears. 'Of course I will.'

'And then you'll never leave me again.'

His voice was thick; startled, Merrin lifted her hands to cup his face, felt it tighten beneath her fingers. She looked up, met the suspicious brightness of his gaze and realised just how much he loved her and needed her.

'No, I'll never leave you,' she said, and kissed him, her mouth as ardent and seeking as ever it had been. 'I love you,' she whispered shakenly a long time later, 'I love you. Never let me go.'

'No, love, never, I swear, I swear it. This time we'll make it. I knew it when I saw you that first night, remember? You sat on the lounger and there were tears on your lashes and I knew then that whatever had happened, I'd get no rest until you were my wife.' He held her closely, all passion spent, only an incredible tenderness left.

Merrin sighed. 'You were an absolute beast to me.'

'Well, I didn't say I was happy about it.'

'Are you happy about it now?' She was laughing, not at all afraid of his answer.

When it came it was not in words, but she knew what he meant.

A WORD ABOUT THE AUTHOR

Robyn Donald is a native New Zealander. She grew up on a dairy farm, met her future husband when she was fifteen, went to Auckland to train as a teacher and then came home to be married.

After the birth of a son, the family moved to Auckland. A little lonely and housebound as she awaited the birth of her daughter, Robyn began the first tentative steps that set her on the path to writing. Her first attempt was, she says, "appallingly bad." But she was determined to keep at it.

Another move took the family to the far north of New Zealand. Robyn returned to teaching but still found time to write; with her husband's encouragement she submitted a manuscript entitled *Bride at Whangatapu*. It was accepted and became Harlequin Presents #232, published in 1978.

For reference, Robyn keeps a file of clippings, jottings of ideas, photographs and a diary, which, she laughingly says, "is useful in my work as well as settling family arguments!"

HARLEQUIN
PREMIERE AUTHOR EDITIONS

6 top Harlequin authors—6 of their best books!

1. **JANET DAILEY** Giant of Mesabi
2. **CHARLOTTE LAMB** Dark Master
3. **ROBERTA LEIGH** Heart of the Lion
4. **ANNE MATHER** Legacy of the Past
5. **ANNE WEALE** Stowaway
6. **VIOLET WINSPEAR** The Burning Sands

Harlequin is proud to offer these 6 exciting romance novels by 6 of our most popular authors. In brand-new beautifully designed covers, each Harlequin Premiere Author Edition is a bestselling love story—a contemporary, compelling and passionate read to remember!

Available wherever paperback books are sold, *or* through Harlequin Reader Service. Simply complete and mail the coupon below.

- -

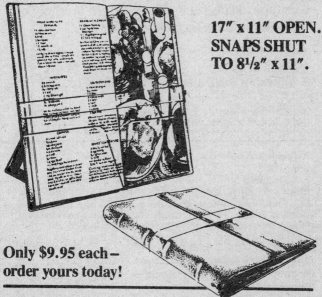